A CHRISTMAS CRUISE

1976. Working in the Purser's Office of a cruise ship, Carys is immersed in a drama with cabaret singer Noah, who witnesses a fight. One passenger falls overboard — but tycoon Rupert, heavily involved in the scuffle, disappears, leaving Noah to report the incident. Carys and Noah form a sleuthing partnership to ensure justice is done. Christmas sparkle is everywhere, while the liner visits idyllic sunny ports, and the friendship turns to something deeper. But will they solve the mystery of the disappearing passenger?

JILL BARRY

◆

A CHRISTMAS CRUISE

Complete and Unabridged

LINFORD
Leicester

First published in Great Britain in 2022 by
D.C. Thomson & Co. Ltd.
Dundee

First Linford Edition
published 2023
by arrangement with
the author and
D.C. Thomson & Co. Ltd.
Dundee

A catalogue record for this book is available
from the British Library.

ISBN 978–1–4448–5185–4

Published by
Ulverscroft Limited
Anstey, Leicestershire

Printed and bound in Great Britain by
TJ Books Ltd., Padstow, Cornwall

This book is printed on acid-free paper

Cinderella

Carys walked fast, dragging her heavy suitcase. She had followed the signs to the ship and felt she must be close now.

'Oh, no!' She struggled to regain her balance. The heel of her right shoe, having come adrift from its upper, lay on the ground beside her.

A jolt from behind left her wobbling again, on the verge of losing not only her balance but also her dignity.

'Hey, watch it!' she called, frowning.

'Whoops!' came a male voice.

He gripped her left arm to steady her.

'I'm so sorry. I was going through some lyrics in my head and walked slap-bang into your suitcase. Are you all right?'

Carys looked up at this handsome stranger and tried to smile.

'I'm sorry, the heel of my shoe snapped so I stopped suddenly. No wonder you bumped into me.'

She bent to retrieve the offending object.

1

'Nice of you to take the blame but you obviously have a problem. Can I help?'

Carys shrugged.

'Not sure, but thanks for offering.'

He took both shoe sections from her.

'I may be able to hammer it back in place. This happened to my sister once while I was with her. Let's see if I still have the knack.'

Carys couldn't help thinking he seemed familiar though she couldn't think why. And why had he been thinking about a song instead of looking where he was going?

She watched him as he put the two parts together, then jumped as he thumped the shoe on the ground.

He handed it back to her before raking the fingers of one hand through his glossy brown hair.

'Try it on, Cinderella.' He smiled at her. 'With any luck it'll hold up long enough to get you to your magic coach. And hopefully you'll have packed plenty of shoes!'

His brown eyes sparkled with humour

2

behind steel-rimmed glasses.

She cleared her throat.

'Thanks so much for your help. I have to report to the crew security gate.'

'Same here. Good luck.'

He waited while she gathered her belongings and set off again. Perfect manners.

Carys wished she'd introduced herself and discovered his name or even what his onboard job was but it was too late now.

She was almost at the barrier, her tummy lurching. What, previously, she'd only dreamed of was really happening!

She was close enough to the gleaming white liner to see movement on deck.

The two young women ahead of her seemed very animated about something and she couldn't avoid overhearing their conversation.

'Would you believe I saw him getting out of a taxi and asking someone if he was in the right place?' The blonde girl laughed.

'You couldn't mistake those cool

specs he wears when he's not performing. Glasses or not, he's still gorgeous,' she finished wistfully.

'I haven't read anything about Noah joining the ship, though. Have you?' her companion replied. 'You'd think there'd be something in the papers after all those rave reviews for 'Angel In Black Leather'.'

Noah. Had this been her shoe-repairing knight?

'Excuse me.'

Carys turned around to face a tall, dark-haired girl.

'Hi! I hope I'm not being too forward,' the stranger said. 'You look so calm. You must have worked on a cruise ship before.'

Carys laughed.

'You couldn't be more wrong. I've completed my training course but I still feel greener than a lettuce. My tummy's turning somersaults as I speak!

'Oh, I'm Carys.'

'Pleased to meet you. I'm Tina; I'm a stewardess. I find it hard to believe I'm back again for maybe my seventh contract! So, what's your job?'

'Purser's Office in the lowliest possible position. It's good to meet you, Tina. Have you travelled far?'

'Only from Bristol, so not too bad. At least the train wasn't late.'

They shuffled forward again.

'I've travelled from Cardiff so not too long a journey for me, either.' Carys looked behind her. 'People are still arriving. Good job the queue's moving quickly.'

'I can't wait to get on board and leave this dismal weather behind,' Tina said.

Carys nodded.

'This will be my first Christmas away from home but I have to admit I can't wait to get away, either.'

'It looks like we'll be aboard soon,' Tina decided. 'I hope we meet again. Maybe have a coffee together some time?'

'I'd like that. I'll keep an eye open for you at meal times.'

'Or in the crew bar,' her new friend said, eyes twinkling. 'Hey, look, it's almost your turn. I hope all goes well for you in your new job.'

Carys showed her proof of employment to the official at the gangway and finally stepped on deck.

She wanted to pinch herself. She was about to begin her dream job and this ship would be her temporary home now.

It was 1976 and she'd be celebrating Christmas in the tropics this year. How amazing was that?

A pang shot through her as she thought of her family. Still, Carys's elder brother would be collecting their parents on Christmas Eve and taking them to his family's house.

Their mum and dad would be chuffed to bits at having the perfect excuse to spoil their grandchildren.

Meanwhile, it was time to go through necessary procedures. Carys concentrated hard while she and others were given basic safety instructions before going any further.

* * *

Carys let herself into her cabin to find her luggage already there.

Looking around, she decided the best word to describe her accommodation was snug but all appeared in immaculate order and the bed linen looked crisp and inviting.

She kicked off her high heels, stooping to pick up the troublemaker. She doubted she'd find a cobbler on board but, as Noah had speculated, she'd definitely packed too many shoes!

Once in her uniform, checking her reflection in the mirror, Carys hardly recognised the young woman staring back.

It was time she set off for her first team meeting. Would she find her way back to the right deck without getting lost?

This thought was enough to propel her through her door and out into the narrow corridor.

First Day

The chief purser rose to survey his staff, some of whom were chatting. Carys envied their relaxed manner.

She was still surprised to arrive in the right place, though still felt as if she was dreaming.

'Welcome,' he said. 'For our two new-comers, I'm Andy Barnes. If you haven't worked with me before be assured many of your colleagues have. The fact they are back here today proves they're either deluded or they need the money desperately!'

He grinned at the two new crew members as his team chuckled.

Andy reminded them of the importance of the safety drills and wished them all a happy voyage.

'I'd advise you all to get a cup of tea and a bite to eat before the hordes arrive. The passengers begin boarding at one p.m. so you have time to refresh yourselves before the fun starts.'

He consulted his clipboard.

'Carys Lloyd-Smith?' He nodded at her. 'I'm putting you with Mark Thornberry. Mark has has worked with me before and he'll guide you through everything.'

He nodded at Mark.

'Happy with that?'

'Very happy.'

Andy raised his eyebrows and everyone laughed. Carys was blushing but they seemed a good-hearted lot. She noticed Mark was looking pink, too. That cheered her up tremendously.

She walked to the crew cafeteria with her mentor, chatting about what they'd done before joining the cruise company.

Mark had worked at Heathrow Airport for a major airline while Carys had been with a well-known hotel chain. Suddenly the butterflies in hob-nailed boots had ceased stomping around her tummy.

Mark smiled at her as they were on their second cup of tea.

'I know you're nervous — we all are

when beginning a new rôle — but with your hotel experience you'll be fine. I'm sure the personnel department was delighted to appoint you.'

'Nice of you to say so but I'll be glad when my first day's over.'

'We'll try to make it as easy as possible. You've joined a friendly team. Most of us have worked on this ship before which is always helpful.'

Mark continued to chatter and make her laugh and Carys felt that she had made a new buddy.

He told her his girlfriend worked in the liner's beauty salon and confided his plan to propose to her during the voyage.

Carys promised not to breathe a word to anyone.

'Have you bought the ring?' she asked, smiling.

'Do you know, I wondered about it, but she's a very independent-minded lady. I thought instead, provided she says yes . . .'

'Which I'm sure she will!' Carys interjected.

He laughed.

'I thought we could go ashore, maybe at the port where we'll spend Christmas, and see if we can buy the ring there.'

Christmas. Carys had left gifts for her family, wrapped in bright paper and tied up with sparkling tinsel, safely in her mum's care.

At the moment she couldn't even recall where the ship would dock for Christmas Eve and the big day itself.

Still, she was here now and her new job demanded full concentration.

Privileged Passengers

Back at Reception, with phones ringing and people moving around, Carys felt a buzz yet began to relax.

She earned an approving comment or two from Mark and, thankfully, people didn't seem to mind her asking questions.

When a voice boomed over the loud-speaker system, announcing their departure, she was thrilled. Her first voyage!

Would this be the first of many or would she fail to make the grade once the excitement dissolved and her colleagues' patience ran out?

She glanced up at the next person to arrive at the desk and, suddenly, it was as though the sun had come out.

'Fancy seeing you here.' Her rescuer stood before her, smiling.

Carys swallowed hard.

'Hi, yourself.'

To her dismay she couldn't remember his name. She also regretted greeting him so casually and hoped Mark hadn't overheard.

She still wasn't sure if this young man really was the celebrity the girls in the boarding queue had talked about.

'I'm grateful for your help on the quayside,' she told him. 'You helped me out of an awkward situation.'

He was studying her name badge.

'Carys? A beautiful name. I'm Noah.'

Her pulse raced as he treated her to a lazy smile. Concentrate, she scolded herself.

'What can I do for you, Mr — I mean, Noah? How's your cabin?'

'Great. I need to find the entertainments director and the gang. Can you point me in the right direction, please?'

So he really was a famous singer, even if she hadn't remembered his name! Carys consulted her list. Now she also recalled his surname was Darcy.

'Room 22. There's a deck plan on the wall over there.' She pointed to it. 'If you prefer I can ask someone to take you there.'

He shook his head.

'I'll leave a trail of crumbs on my way, just in case.' That smile again. 'Better get out of your hair.

'Thanks for your help, Carys. See you.'

She watched him examine the deck plan then head for the door. He seemed pleasant and funny. She'd met celebrities in her former job and not all were as friendly.

She turned her attention to a smartly dressed couple approaching the desk.

'Good afternoon and welcome aboard.'

She smiled at the tall, ugly yet attractive man and his young, glamorous companion.

'May I take your names, please?'

'Afternoon. Rupert Maitland and wife.'

'I'm Summer Maitland,' his wife stated.

She wore a red fox fur cape over a chocolate-brown trouser suit.

Her hand was on the desk, sporting a diamond-and-emerald engagement ring alongside her wedding band.

Mr Maitland gave Carys a hard stare.

'My PA reserved your most luxurious suite so I trust all is in order.'

'I'm sure it will be, sir.'

Carys ran her finger down the passenger list and swiftly found *Maitland x 2*. Something about this man told her he expected instant attention.

'You're in Penthouse Number One on the top deck, Mr Maitland. Your luggage awaits you.' She turned to his wife. 'Your suite has a private balcony.'

Carys handed them gold-tagged doorkeys.

'You can take the elevator but it's no great distance to walk.'

'I dislike stairs.' Rupert Maitland glanced at her name badge. 'May we order English tea and sandwiches to be brought to our suite, um, Carys?'

Carys hesitated. She felt certain they could but hadn't yet met with that request.

Luckily Mark leaned across.

'You can, sir. Your steward or stewardess will be waiting to greet you and will

15

explain the many services we offer.'

The tall man nodded.

'Excellent. Thank you, young man — and you, Carys. I can sense you're new to this but I'm sure you'll be fine.'

He turned to his wife.

'Let's go and settle in, my darling.'

His wife tossed back her mane of copper hair, gave Carys an appraising stare then took Rupert's arm before sashaying off on her crocodile-skin stilettos.

Carys realised now who she was. She wrote as Summer Breeze, a journalist whose column appeared in Carys's parents' favourite Sunday paper. She also contributed features to one or two of the glossy magazines Carys's mum loved.

Her fame rose from her interrogation skills and ability to coax the most reluctant of film stars into answering questions. Her romantic adventures mostly involved a succession of rich, handsome escorts from the worlds of finance and cinema.

Rupert Maitland qualified as wealthy

but he was hardly heartthrob material. Summer must have found true love at last.

No Business Like It

Noah found the door of Room 22 half open so he went straight in. At once he sensed the heady mix of excitement and panic accompanying first-night preparations.

At the same time he thought about how much he loved show business.

One man strode forward, hand outstretched.

'Noah! Great to see you again. I think you know most people but since our last rehearsal we've made a couple of replacements.

'Fortunately our new cast members are quick learners.'

Noah shook hands with the director he'd worked with in London in preparation for this cruise. Already he'd spotted the newcomers although both their faces seemed familiar.

The director called for attention.

'OK, guys. Suki and Liam? I realise Noah Darcy needs no introduction but he'll come over and say hi while I'm looking through his music.

'Dancers, you can start your warm up. Our dance captain will put you through your paces. It's a simple routine with glamorous costumes galore!

'You'll have scope to show off your multitude of skills as the cruise progresses.'

Noah handed over his music and headed towards the new male vocalist. After a brief chat with him he spoke to the singers and dancers who'd be working with him throughout the cruise.

The second replacement vocalist, Suki, was a girl he'd known at music college. They had some mutual friends.

She gave him a hug.

'I knew I'd catch up with you one day, honey,' she told him. 'It's fantastic you're doing so well but I was sorry to hear about you and Georgie breaking up.'

Noah shrugged. Something told him Suki wasn't the least bit sorry.

'It was a difficult situation,' he admitted, 'acting out an on-stage romance after being in a relationship for a year, then ending it.

'I decided, for both our sakes, to leave the cast.' He kissed her cheek. 'Great to see you again, Suki. We must catch up soon.'

'We'll have plenty of time, Noah. These ships are floating prisons!' The beautiful, coffee-skinned singer smiled up at him.

'A luxurious prison like this sounds good to me. Looking forward to seeing something of the Caribbean, too.'

Suki gave him a kiss and moved off to join the other vocalists.

Noah frowned. He had no intention of discussing his former relationship with anybody. For now it was enough to be with people who understood each other's life style.

Showbusiness was a precarious way to earn a living and Noah, though much in demand at present, was aware of the potential swift slide into obscurity should his popularity wane.

His agent had been furious when her

star client first announced his news.

'You what?' Sadie had spluttered when he had visited her Covent Garden office. 'Work on a cruise liner when I can get you a choice of rôles coming up in the next few weeks? Are you out of your mind?'

He had told her he needed a break from London. She had countered that with insisting he could escape from the Capital by accepting the lead in the touring version of 'Devilish Delights' which would be opening in Glasgow the following month.

'You'd be perfect for the rôle of Prime Minister!' she had wailed as he shook his head. 'The promotor would bite my hand off to get you!'

'I'm sorry, Sadie. I want you to find me a good spot on a luxurious liner. Nothing too enormous but one that will keep me out of touch for several weeks.

'After that I promise to come back to London.'

His agent had muttered and grumbled

21

but had come up with *The Golden Goddess*.

Medium-sized, and with a cruise itinerary to die for, its ports of call included Marquisa and several other exotic-sounding resorts as it sailed to Barbados.

The ship wouldn't dock back at Southampton until New Year.

Noah anticipated luxury he wouldn't normally enjoy plus time ashore to explore tropical islands totally alien to a lad from Northampton.

He joined the rest of the group and was soon doing some vocal warm-ups.

Suddenly he thought of the pretty girl with the honey-coloured hair into whom he had bumped twice already.

After almost falling over her and then finding her again Noah decided he needed another excuse to call at Reception.

Time for Tea

Once the check-in rush ended Carys longed for a cup of tea, and was grateful when her turn came for a break.

On the way to the crew mess, she didn't think she'd made any glaring errors, or upset any passengers. She still couldn't believe how busy it had been.

One of her new colleagues, Suzanne, came over, eager to ask how she got on with Mr and Mrs Maitland, the VIPs.

'Summer is his third wife. It's obvious why she's married him — he's worth a fortune so she'll never again want for anything! She'll be able to give up work if she wants.

'What did you make of her, Carys?'

'I wasn't with her for long but I'd be surprised if she wasn't in love with him. People marry other people for all kinds of reasons, don't they?

'It's clear Summer's a lot younger than her husband but she has a good career and I hope she'll continue with it.'

'Are you a bit of a Women's Libber, then?' Suzanne pressed.

'Not especially. I just don't see why women can't have a successful career whether married or single if they wish.

'If we can believe the gossip columns Summer has had loads of boyfriends, most of them rolling in money. Wouldn't she have chosen one of them if marriage really was her only goal?'

Suzanne shrugged.

'Let's get a cup of tea and you can tell me how you got on. I doubt you'll be expected to work for much longer today.

'Andy's very fair to his staff and he's good to work for.'

'I don't mind,' Carys replied. 'I can do with all the practice I can get!'

Suzanne chuckled.

'You'll be shattered by the time you get back to your cabin. Take my advice and have something to eat before you do that.'

She nudged Carys.

'Speaking of celebrities I've met plenty in my time but never one as gorgeous as

24

Noah Darcy. Have you seen him?'

'He came to the desk asking where to find the Musical Director.'

'And?' Suzanne's eyes sparkled.

'And he left. He seemed nice enough.'

Carys wondered why she was reluctant to mention the quayside incident. Whatever the reason she decided to keep that first meeting to herself.

Fine Dining

The cruise company encouraged the purser's staff to mingle with the passengers whenever possible, including joining them for meals.

Upon going off duty Carys was grateful when Suzanne took her under her wing and marched her off to the Rococo Restaurant.

The maître d' seated them at a table for six where two couples were already into their starters. They were introduced but Carys immediately forgot their names.

At this point she would have happily settled for beans on toast in her cabin but she told herself not to be stupid. Folk paid a lot for their cruise and she was lucky to be heading away from chilly, fog-draped England to winter sunshine.

She must enjoy every new experience.

'How long have you worked for the cruise company?' Mr Silver Hair asked.

'This is my first job in the Purser's Office,' Carys confessed.

'Several years,' Suzanne said. 'Each voyage is different from the one before. It's fascinating how the dynamics change.'

'What kind of cruise will this one be, I wonder,' Mrs Silver Hair said, smiling.

'A peaceful one, I hope!' Suzanne said. 'Calm seas and happy passengers would be great for my first time,' Carys admitted.

'Well, I'm looking forward to sparkling stage shows and mountains of delicious food!' Mr Ruffled Evening Shirt chimed in.

'Always thinking of his stomach.' Mrs Ruffled Evening Shirt laughed. 'As for me I'm looking forward to not getting up at five to put the turkey in on Christmas Day!'

Just then a ripple of interest shimmered through the nearby diners. She looked over and saw Rupert and Summer Maitland taking their seats.

Rupert looked much better when in evening dress. Summer, radiant in a jade-green, sequinned cocktail dress, would probably have looked ravishing in a sack!

Conversation at her table dried up until her colleague enquired whether anyone had visited Barbados before. As Mr Silver Hair began talking about volcanic landscapes Carys glanced at the next table.

Rupert was talking to the wine waiter while his wife studied the menu. Summer's glorious hair caught the light as she glanced up at her fellow-diners, smiling and nodding to those trying to catch her eye.

Carys was enjoying a slice of Black Forest gateau when Mrs Ruffled Evening Shirt asked if she was a fan of Noah Darcy.

'I'm so thrilled he's top of the entertainments bill!' she confessed.

Carys racked her brain for the name of the show in which Noah had recently starred.

'I hear he was brilliant in 'Angel In Black Leather'.'

'True. I saw it with my daughter,' Mrs

Ruffled Evening Shirt told her. 'She'll be so jealous when she hears he's on this ship. Such a talented young man, and so handsome. He'll probably need a bodyguard with so many glamorous divorcees and widows on board!

'Have you met him yet, dear?'

'Yes, earlier today.'

Carys knew she mustn't discuss any of the passengers no matter who asked.

'Ooh, lucky girl! I think Noah has a superb voice and a lovely personality.'

Across the table Suzanne was raising her eyebrows. Carys took the hint and nodded.

Suzanne pushed back her chair.

'Please excuse us, ladies and gentlemen. It's time Carys and I made a move.'

'Do you have to get back to work?' Mrs Silver Hair asked.

'Just for a while. Enjoy the rest of the evening.' She turned to Carys. 'Ready?'

'Yes, thanks. It's lovely to have met you all. You've given me the perfect ending to my first day on duty.'

'You made a good impression,'

Suzanne told Carys as they left. 'I heard Mrs Saunders say what a lovely girl you were and how she'd enjoyed talking to you.'

'I forgot their names almost as soon as I heard them! Isn't that awful?'

'It's hard at first but it's important to remember who everyone is.

'Now, how about a nightcap in the crew bar? That'll round off your first day nicely.'

★ ★ ★

Noah stood in the doorway of the crew bar and glanced around, searching for familiar faces.

He was used to people staring at him but, to his relief, these people only gave him a glance or a smile then resumed chatting.

He spotted someone waving from a corner table near the bar and, realising who it was, went over.

'Hi, Suki. Can I get you two another drink?'

He smiled at Suki's companion who was another of the ensemble. The young man got to his feet.

'We're fine, thanks, but what would you like, Noah? Let me buy you one while you catch up with Suki.'

'If you insist I'd like a half of lager, please. It's Steve, isn't it?'

'Yep, that's me.' He set off for the bar.

'Steve seems a nice guy. Have you worked with him before?' Noah asked, settling himself.

'We did a couple of Mediterranean cruises together earlier this year.'

Suki stared at him.

'I can't believe you decided to join *The Golden Goddess*. Why a cruise?'

'Why not? You're not telling me this ship is jinxed, are you?' he replied lightly.

'Of course not. It's only that I'm surprised you haven't been snapped up for a new West End show.'

Noah shrugged.

'My agent's still barely speaking to me but I had to move on. Not just stop playing the Angel but leave London.

'I'd have thought you'd understand.'

She squeezed his hand before leaning closer to kiss his cheek.

'Of course I understand. It must have been a constant strain, playing love scenes with Georgie after you two split up.'

Noah was still in deep conversation with Suki when Steve returned with his drink.

None of them noticed two young women in uniform walking towards the counter.

Strange Request

Next morning Carys tried not to picture the little scene at the crew bar the night before. Noah had seemed to have been enjoying the attentions of his female companion.

What did she expect? A star like Noah Darcy would have admirers worldwide.

'Good morning, um, Carys.'

She spun round to face Rupert Maitland who was immaculate in polo shirt and chinos and was carrying a jacket.

'Good morning, sir. I'm so sorry, I didn't notice you arriving.'

'No problem, my dear. I'm about to take a turn on deck but I wonder if you could satisfy my curiosity.'

'I'll try my best. How can I help you, Mr Maitland?'

He rested one arm on the counter and leaned in.

'It's only that, last night, I thought I glimpsed someone I used to know.

'I went up on deck for a stroll before

turning in and this man was some way away, but I saw his profile beneath a light before he disappeared.

'I wonder, is there a man called Simon Waters on the passenger list?'

Carys felt a ripple of anxiety. How was she supposed to deal with this request when she was forbidden to divulge information about other passengers?

Unfortunately Mark was occupied with two elderly ladies at the other end of the counter.

'I'm very sorry, sir, but I'm not permitted to reveal passenger information.'

Ignoring his obvious irritation she preempted any argument by mentioning the chief purser.

'My boss is away from his office but if you could come back a little later you can speak to him personally. Would that be OK, sir?'

'It'll have to be, won't it? Sorry, young lady, I know you're only doing your job. Perhaps you could mention my request to your chief on his return.

'Tell him who was asking, eh?'

There was no smile for her this time as Rupert slipped his arms into his jacket before turning and heading for the door like a ship surging through the waves.

Carys returned to what she'd been doing. She knew she had upset the tycoon but there was no way she could risk disobeying the rules.

The moment Mark became free she explained to him what had happened and how awkward she felt.

'It seemed a harmless enough request, you see. I hope Mr Maitland wasn't too offended but I'd have got into trouble, wouldn't I?'

To her surprise her colleague didn't fully agree.

'Technically you were right, Carys. It's a pity I was busy but what's done is done and you mustn't worry about it.

'Tell Andy as soon as he gets here and, when Maitland comes back, we'll have an answer ready.'

'Thanks, Mark.'

She spotted someone waiting and greeted them, pleased this time at being able to offer assistance without checking with her colleague.

As soon as the chief purser arrived Carys asked if she could have a word.

He ushered her into his office where she explained her dilemma, explaining that Mark had been busy at the time so she had done what she thought was right.

'I see. Well, Carys, you were absolutely spot on,' Andy told her.

Carys smiled, relieved.

'However, and I hate to say this, we need to bear in mind Rupert is an important customer of the company which employs you and me.

'He expects nothing less than top-class service, whether it's the quality of the hot breakfast rolls or the pillows on his bed.

'So he should, mind, given he's paying top whack — even though some would say that with his income he can afford to travel the world in luxury.

'What was the name of the man he wondered about?'

'Simon Waters.'

Andy picked up a folder.

'We've no idea which part of the ship his cabin's in but that won't take long to check. When Mr Maitland returns you'll have the answer.

'Better let Mark know as well, in case you're busy when our friend returns.'

The chief's phone rang so he pushed the typewritten sheets across his desk to her.

'You can start checking now.'

Carys began with the list of passengers booked into inside cabins, going immediately to the letter 'W' and noting examining the surnames. Then she moved to the cabins whose portholes faced the outside of the ship.

After checking she still hadn't found the surname Rupert had mentioned.

Andy was ending his call.

'Any luck?'

'It seems he was mistaken.'

'As a matter of interest did he seem eager to be proved right or did he look worried?'

37

Carys considered.

'Mr Maitland didn't look too happy but he was OK about my refusing his request.'

'Good.' Andy tapped his pen against his teeth. 'There is another possibility. If Maitland did see this Simon Waters last night the guy must be using a false name.

'In other words he might be travelling with false documentation. Men like Maitland make lots of friends but they also have plenty of enemies.'

'Goodness! You're not suggesting this person is out to rob the Maitlands!'

Andy shrugged.

'Who knows? It may be the man has some hold on him or even a grudge.'

He glanced at his watch.

'I have a meeting. Don't worry about this, Carys, I'm probably jumping to conclusions. The man our esteemed guest thought he saw happened to bear a fleeting resemblance to one Simon Waters.

'After all, this didn't happen in daylight.'

Later Carys was looking at information about excursions ashore when Rupert and Summer appeared.

'Any luck?' Rupert raised his eyebrows.

'I'm sorry, sir. I spoke to the chief and we did a thorough check but there's nobody on board with the name you mention.'

He stared at her for a moment before nodding as if relieved.

'Well, that's good to hear. I must have had one too many brandies after last night's excellent dinner. Thank you for attending to my request so promptly, er, Carys.'

He moved aside and his wife took his place, looking at Carys with a little smile.

'No idea what that was all about, darling. Now, we were wondering how to spend our time ashore at the first port of call after Marquisa.'

'Did you want to stay the night there before returning to the ship?'

'That's a thought.'

'I'll be pleased to help you, Mrs Maitland. Do you have a favourite hotel in Porto Claro or would you like me to do some research and get back to you?'

'The latter, please. My husband enjoys a round of golf so if you could bear that in mind you'd make him even happier a man than he already is.

'While he's occupied on the links I might sample one of those volcanic mud baths they say are so beneficial.'

'I'll check on those as well.'

'Thank you. I'll call back later.'

Summer moved towards her husband and took his arm.

The image of the big man with his glamorous wife was one Carys thought she wouldn't forget in a hurry. Their lifestyle was so very different from that of hers or anyone else she knew.

As the couple strolled towards the escalator Carys wondered why Rupert had seemed so pleased — relieved, even — about her failure to find the missing man.

Maybe he was happy keeping a low profile or did he have something to fear from Simon Waters?

It hardly seemed possible someone in his position could be vulnerable but who was she to comment?

It was only later, when taking her break, that Carys thought of yet another possibility. What if the person Rupert knew had signed on as crew?

Neither she nor the chief purser had checked the crew list. She might even have typed that name on it herself without a thought.

For whatever reason it seemed his presence — or absence — was important to Rupert Maitland.

Scoop!

Appearing in the musical 'Angel In Black Leather' had led to Noah being invited to appear on TV and radio chat shows.

Now, instead of having girls crowding round the stage door, Noah stood poised to perform predominantly for silver-haired cruise-ship passengers.

His first performance would take place that evening in the music lounge. The songs consisted mainly of his personal favourites and he would be supported by four backing singers including Suki.

While he was pleased to see her again Noah feared she might try to become too close to him. He didn't need that.

There had already been too many emotions flying around in those last weeks with his former girlfriend, starring together on stage and sparring off it.

Today's afternoon rehearsal hadn't gone well though Noah knew that, often, a disastrous dress rehearsal heralded a triumphant first night.

He grabbed his fleecy jacket and set off to walk on deck. He saw a tall figure, wrapped up against the chilly weather, walking towards him.

She stopped and gave him a huge smile.

'Hi! I'm Summer Maitland, Mr Darcy. We haven't met but I want to say how much my husband and I loved your performance in the West End the other week.'

'My swan song, you mean? Oh, don't worry, Mrs Maitland. I decided not to continue in the show because I needed to get out of the line of fire.'

She chuckled and they moved towards a sheltered part of the deck.

'Call me Summer. I know the feeling but right now you're on a ship surrounded by scores of adoring females! Hardly a rest cure, is it, darling?'

She gazed at the sullen sky.

'Oh, I'll be glad to reach warmer climes!'

'True. But the fans are important, aren't they? If nobody cared whether I sang or not my career would be over. Imagine if all your readers stopped reading your articles.'

Summer shrugged.

'I see you know who I am. Actually, darling, I wonder whether I could interview you for my Sunday-paper column while we're both all at sea, so to speak?

'I know it's a frightful cheek, asking you like this, but my editor would be ecstatic.'

Noah knew no publicity was bad publicity but felt doubtful.

'I will discuss my career but I don't intend talking about my personal life. I'm sure the newspapers have raked over my broken romance till everyone must be tired of hearing about it.'

She nodded.

'Understood. Nevertheless I suspect I might have a scoop if I'm the first to interview you since you left London.'

'You definitely will have. I've no intention of sharing my secrets with anybody else, not even a passing seagull with a mini tape recorder strapped to his neck!'

44

Laughing, Summer gave him a hug.

'We'll keep this secret between the two of us. When's a good time for you to visit the penthouse? We can't meet in one of the lounges without attracting attention.'

'I guess not. My days revolve around rehearsing and performing but I do get several hours off in the afternoon.

'Things are still hectic as we're rehearsing our new show. Maybe in a few days' time?'

'Great. How about Saturday at three o'clock? Rupert's found a little card school so we'll have the place to ourselves. Now, shall we keep moving before I freeze to the deck?'

She linked arms with him and they set off in the direction she'd been heading. Noah was too good-natured to point out he'd been walking the opposite way.

From the corner of his eye he noticed a man dressed in dark clothing standing at the nearby rail.

He wondered if the guy had overheard the conversation.

Might he also be a journalist, jealous

about Summer jumping in with an interview request?

Noah was what the tabloids described as 'squeaky-clean'. It was a quality fans loved him for and he had learned early on not to trust everyone he came across within the entertainment world.

After Summer left him to visit the shops he hastened back to the spot where she and he had chatted.

If the man he had noticed was still around maybe he and Noah could have a conversation. He could find out if the guy was harmless and had merely been enjoying the bracing air.

But he looked around in vain. Whether a journalist or not, the mysterious man in black was nowhere to be seen.

Making Friends

By the fifth day at sea Carys felt the hours were flying by too quickly. She said so next day at lunch in the crew mess with Tina, the stewardess she had met on their first day.

'Anyone can tell you're a newbie!' Tina teased as they queued for their meals. 'You'll soon be glad to see the days whizz by, especially as we near the end of the voyage.'

Carys didn't argue.

'Well, you're the expert.'

'An old hand, you mean!' Tina eyed the dishes on offer. 'It's lovely to see you again but I hope you're not tired already of eating with the passengers?'

'No, but I want to make the most of all the opportunities I'm given. I'm glad I ran into you. I hope they've given you a good set of passengers to look after.'

'It's early days but everything's fine so far. I have the responsibility of looking after Rupert and Summer Maitland, arguably the most important VIPs on board.'

'I know, and staying in the most superior of the penthouses! I'm not sure about Mr Maitland but Summer seems lovely.'

'My mother reads her Sunday column and I remember her telling me about Summer being on Concorde's first commercial flight from Heathrow.'

'Gosh, I must ask her what she thought of it. I do admire the way she follows her own career and doesn't trail along in her husband's wake.'

'So far Rupert Maitland's fine with me but I try to be unobtrusive.' Tina chuckled. 'Unlike you, in full view of everyone!'

'I think wearing the uniform helps build my confidence and the team's great. I get on well with Mark and Suzanne and Andy's a lovely man. I wish my former boss had been half as good to work for!'

To her surprise Tina didn't respond. They reached the serving area and carried plates of fish and chips and slices of lemon-meringue pie to a nearby table.

After sitting down Carys broke the silence.

'Have I said something to offend you?'

Tina shook her head.

'No. It's just that Andy and I have been seeing one another away from the ship.

'Before our last cruise ended he asked if we might meet up during our leave.

'He explained he'd been plucking up courage to ask me out for the last three months! It seems he got divorced after his ex-wife couldn't handle his absences at sea.

'Anyway, I've always enjoyed his company so I said yes. But Carys, we're hoping to keep this quiet for now.'

'Your secret's safe with me,' Carys assured her. 'I hope you manage to get some time together now you're on board!'

'To be honest, when you said what a lovely man he is I was afraid you might be attracted to him.'

'No way! I think Andy's great; good-looking, too. But truly, Tina, I'm not interested in him — or anyone else.'

She banished the image of Noah Darcy from her mind's eye. As if he'd want her anyway!

Tina speared another chip.

'Well, this is the real thing for me. I just hope it is for him.'

'It sounds promising. I'm pleased for you both.'

'Thanks. Carys, I hope you're not running away to sea to forget any troubles. Some do, but Andy says it's never worth doing that because whatever's bothering you will still haunt you.'

Carys smiled.

'I'm here because I've always fancied working on a cruise ship.'

'What did you do before?'

'I worked for a big hotel chain. I enjoyed the challenge and the travelling but it became something of a rat race.

'This is a chance to see something of the world, even if only in small bites.'

Tina was about to take another bite of lemon-meringue pie when she froze, spoon halfway to her mouth.

'Wow! I don't take much notice of celebrities on board but he is something!'

Carys glanced towards the door. Noah was walking towards the food counter accompanied by the attractive, raven-haired girl who'd been cosying up to him in the crew bar the previous evening.

The sudden way her hands were becoming clammy and her throat was drying confirmed her suspicions.

She must now accept that that first spark of something unexpected on the quayside wasn't going away.

Why on earth did she have to fall for the most attractive man on board *The Golden Goddess*?

The Witching Hour

Back at Reception Carys noticed Rupert Maitland heading towards her.

'Yes, sir?'

She always felt as if she should stand to attention, as if she was back in school and being reprimanded. This man had that kind of effect on her.

Right now, however, he looked as though he was the one up in front of the head teacher.

'I'm afraid I have to bother you again, Carys. I wonder . . .

'Oh, I know this is a long shot and probably stupid of me but could you ask the purser if someone could check the crew names, please?

'The fact is, I'm still wondering if my eyes were deceiving me as to whether or not I'd seen someone I knew . . .' His voice tailed off again.

'I'll check for you, sir,' Carys replied. 'The chief purser is in his office at the moment.'

She tapped on Andy's door and, hearing him respond, slipped inside, closing the door behind her.

'I did wonder if we should check the crew list,' she admitted, 'but I wasn't sure if we'd be allowed to disclose someone's name.'

Andy sighed.

'I wouldn't normally go along with this as it is striking me as being somewhat obsessive.

'Given who it is, though, I'm prepared to check for myself. Leave it with me and please tell Mr Maitland I'll speak to him personally once I'm in possession of the information.

'In fact, I'll get on with it now. Could you tell him he can wait if he wishes?'

'Thanks, Andy.'

Rupert was standing with his back to the Reception Desk, gazing through the window overlooking the deck.

Carys went over to him.

'The Purser sends his compliments, sir. He asked me to tell you that, if you'd care to wait, he'll come and see you once he's checked.'

Rupert hesitated.

'It shouldn't take long,' she added.

She wondered again why Rupert Maitland was so bothered about knowing whether this chap Simon was on board.

He couldn't be a close friend. Didn't buddies usually share their holiday plans with each other?

Something didn't seem right.

While Carys dealt with passengers the Purser emerged from his office and approached Rupert. The two shook hands but she was too busy to notice the big man's reaction.

Later, when Andy told her that nobody of the name in question had been listed as crew, neither of them considered the possibility of Mr Waters using an assumed name.

★ ★ ★

Noah was standing before an audience, performing one of his favourite songs.

He sang with such feeling that Carys,

54

who was standing at the back, noticed several people wiping their eyes.

She thought that the star gave her a little smile before beginning his next song but scolded herself immediately for imagining things.

A romantic number received a rapturous reception and Noah followed it with 'Save Your Kisses For Me'.

As this song had won the Eurovision Song Contest for the UK earlier that year Noah's bouncy rendition was met with much clapping and cheering.

It wasn't until the singer closed his act with a smoochy blues classic that Carys noticed the Maitlands, seated near the front of the lounge.

Summer was looking sensational as usual, with her lustrous hair gleaming under the lights.

She was wearing a figure-hugging gown in buttercup-yellow jersey and Carys couldn't miss Rupert's proud expression as he took her hand to walk her from the lounge.

She slipped out in their wake and she

was intrigued to see Rupert kiss his wife on the cheek, then stand back as she entered the elevator.

He moved away the moment the doors closed and the last she saw of him was his rear view as he headed out on deck.

For some reason Carys glanced at her watch, noticing it was almost midnight, the witching hour.

Why had that popped into her mind? Suddenly, despite the milder weather, Carys shivered.

A Fatal Confrontation

Simon Waters, whose travel documents claimed he was Martin Cooper, watched his former boss head towards the deck.

He pulled up the hood of his black parka, his heart bumping fast, and went outside. This was the perfect moment.

Bent on revenge, Simon checked no-one was around as he approached the man who had ruined his career.

He had dreamed of this confrontation for months. There had been a contact of his who was still working for Rupert's company. He happened to be friendly with the chairman's private secretary.

She had confided the information Simon needed during one morning-coffee break.

Once he had known the Maitlands' plans and sailing date Simon had booked a place on the same cruise though in less sumptuous accommodation.

He found his quarry standing near the

rail, staring up at the night sky. Simon took a deep breath as he padded towards him.

Closer, closer . . .

'Good evening, Rupert.'

Maitland swung round and shaded his eyes against the light glaring from above.

'Great Scott! Why are you creeping up on me like that?'

He distanced himself from the rail swiftly upon recognising him.

'You! I felt sure it was you I'd seen but the purser's office insisted there was no Simon Waters on board.'

'Because I'm using an assumed name.'

Rupert gasped.

'How on earth did you know I was on this cruise?'

Like a cut-out stage prop the moon sailed back into view while clouds shifted away.

Simon smiled.

'Does it matter? I believe you spotted me soon after we sailed. Careless of me, not keeping a safe distance while I was still getting my bearings.'

58

He jabbed Rupert in the chest with his forefinger.

'You caused me to spend a lot of time in my cabin. I had to pretend my back was playing up and have meals delivered to be on the safe side!

'I wanted to give you time to decide that you had been mistaken in believing I was on board.'

'This is ludicrous!' Rupert cried. 'Our association ended months ago and you should have learned to keep your mouth shut. What do you want?

'Someone from the company must have broken confidentiality rules. Whoever it is will pay when I discover the culprit.

'It's unbelievable you should go to such lengths!'

Simon's face was contorted with anger.

'Really? When you destroyed my reputation after my years of loyal service as company secretary?

'I'll tell you what I want, Rupert. You and your financial director were swindling the shareholders and you had it in

59

for me after I discovered your fraudulent behaviour.

'Well, I won't be fobbed off this time. You're going to pay the full amount of money owed to us all and then I shan't bother you again.'

'What if I don't agree?'

'Your lovely wife will be made aware of your, er, misdemeanours, financial and otherwise.'

Simon smiled grimly.

'Once she hears that I took the trouble to join this cruise she will realise I mean business.'

'How dare you?' Rupert hissed. 'I could report you for intimidation and actual bodily harm. There's no way you can prove I was up to anything wrong so just get away from me!

'What you're demanding isn't going to happen so you might as well shut up and enjoy the cruise, though I'd advise you to keep out of my sight!'

Simon hesitated and Rupert backed away from him, keeping a safe distance from the ship's rail.

Suddenly Simon, standing on tip-toe, launched himself forward, his arms outstretched to grab Rupert.

As the older man moved, too, as if to intercept him, a sudden pitching of the liner sent him staggering sideways and he reached for Simon without success.

The momentum created by the younger man lunging angrily at the tycoon drove Simon upward and forward.

Rupert couldn't prevent his assailant from diving past him and toppling, his arms flailing, head first over the ship's rail.

An outburst of merriment from passengers somewhere above blotted out any scream that may have been made.

Nor could Rupert hear the sound of a body plunging into the unforgiving dark sea as he stood, both hands gripping the ship's rail.

Man Overboard!

His performance over, Noah removed his stage makeup and changed into casual clothes. He needed fresh air and made his way to the nearest viewing balcony where he opened the connecting door.

At once he heard voices from the deck below and, looking down, he saw two men.

Their discussion became heated. Noah heard most of it though he lost a few phrases because of the blustery wind.

One man was accusing the other of colluding with their financial director to cook the books, then he demanded the other person put matters right — or else.

Next came a scuffling sound. The deep-voiced man sounded stressed as he ordered the other to back off.

This was none of Noah's business but, if the pair started fighting, surely a crew member should be alerted?

The singer moved closer to the railing and looked down, both men now fully in his line of vision.

Noah watched in dismay as the slighter figure lunged towards the big man. The singer gripped the balcony railing as the liner pitched unexpectedly, the movement catching him unawares.

He gasped in dismay on seeing the big man sway sideways, his head tilted so his seemed focused upon Noah, while the other man, propelled by the momentum of his frenzied action, disappeared over the ship's rail.

Noah rushed inside, instinct propelling him towards Reception. To his relief one of the purser's staff was at the desk.

'Man overboard!' Noah skidded to a halt.

Mark wasted no time.

'When and where?'

Noah pointed.

'Just now, back there. I was on the veranda and saw two men on the deck below. They started to fight and I saw one go over the rail.

'Can you stop the ship?'

'Wait here, please, Mr Darcy.' Mark

picked up a phone.

Noah closed his eyes, taking several deep breaths. He stood with his hands clasped as he struggled to take in the enormity of what he'd witnessed.

'Mr Darcy, could you step inside the chief purser's office, please? Mr Barnes would like to ask you some questions.'

'I'm not drunk if that's what you're thinking!'

Noah ran both hands through his hair.

'Don't you understand that we need to turn the ship around? That poor guy might be floating in the sea, trying to keep himself from drowning!'

The chief purser appeared in his doorway.

'Nobody's accusing you of being drunk, Noah. Come and sit down, please. Rest assured we have an emergency procedure that my deputy has set in motion.

'You've received a bad shock. Let's give you a tot of brandy.'

Noah followed Andy into his office.

'Never mind me, what about the man who fell overboard? Are we slowing down?'

Andy shook his head.

'It would take a while to stop a ship this size. We've alerted the emergency services so the search-and-rescue team at Marquisa will be taking prompt action.'

Andy produced a bottle of brandy and a glass from one of his desk drawers and poured a measure of the golden spirit before handing it to the singer.

Noah swigged it down then pulled a face.

'Thanks. I normally don't touch spirits but you're right about me being shocked.

'One minute I was taking a breather, the next I was witnessing what might have been murder!'

'Could you describe exactly what you saw while it's still fresh in your memory?'

Noah did his best. He ended by saying that, just as the body plunged towards the sea, he'd heard a loud burst of laughter from somewhere above.

'That would have prevented me from hearing a scream and obviously it was impossible to hear the sound of someone entering the water.'

He shuddered.

'Poor fellow. I feel so sorry for him! It sounded like he'd been badly treated by the other man after finding something wrong with the company accounts.

'This was an act of revenge that back-fired in my opinion.'

Andy was making notes. He looked up, his expression serious.

'You might be the only eye-witness, Noah — apart from the other passenger involved, of course. The police will board at Marquisa Harbour after we dock around daybreak and they'll take a statement from you.

'Can you describe the passenger who's still on board? If he doesn't come forward anything you can tell the Marquisa police to aid his identification will help enormously.

'It's worrying that he made no attempt to sound the alarm.'

Noah's Statement

Noah knew he'd never sleep if he didn't unwind. He made his way to the crew bar and found a few of the younger men and women there.

He spotted Steve, this time with no sign of Suki. Relieved, he made his way over.

'I wondered if I'd be the only one still wandering around. Can't you sleep, either?'

'Still feeling wide awake, I'm afraid. How did you think tonight went?' Steve asked.

'The audience seemed pleased. We'll see how tomorrow's show goes. Is this your first cruise? It's mine,' Noah confided.

'Same here. The opportunity arose and my agent sorted things out. I bet the cruise line couldn't believe their luck when they got you booked for the top spot!'

Noah shrugged.

'I asked my agent to find me a gig on a liner and this job came up. I'm relieved we're heading for the sunshine, though I'll miss seeing my little nephew and niece on Christmas Day.'

He thought of their mum, his elder sister. He had got her and her husband tickets for the show he was in and she'd been hurrying across Trafalgar Square with him, on their way to meet her husband before the matinée, when the heel of her shoe had come off.

Noah made an emergency repair, as he'd done for Carys.

Tomorrow, he thought. Tomorrow I want to see her.

Then it all came flooding back. Who knew how long the police would keep him?

With passengers going ashore and returning to the ship for their evening's entertainment Carys would have little or no time at all to spend with him. Yet he longed to get to know her better.

Somehow he must find a way.

'Are you certain that's what you heard?'

Noah, up far too early next morning, sat with a plain-clothes detective from Marquisa who could have stepped straight from an American gumshoe movie.

At least some kind person had supplied hot, black coffee.

'I'm positive. I couldn't make out every word because the wind was gusting but the one who fell overboard was pretty agitated.

'He talked about his loyal service as company secretary then insisted he wanted justice for the shareholders.'

Noah frowned.

'He definitely accused his former employer of fraud. It seemed odd that someone would go to the lengths of booking the same cruise as his former boss but I got the impression he did this so he could corner the other guy.

'I also heard him threaten to tell the other man's wife.'

'Would you recognise the older man if you saw him again, sir?'

Noah hesitated.

'He was a big fellow with a deep voice, one I'd know again, but I wasn't leaning over the railing deliberately spying.

'I was taking a breather after the show and couldn't help eavesdropping. It was only when I realised things were turning nasty that I became concerned.

'I'm not sure about recognising the older man. I'm sorry I can't be more helpful. The instant I realised there was a man overboard I rushed off to report it.'

The detective nodded, asked several more questions then put down his notebook.

'We'll get your statement typed up then someone will bring it to the ship and we'll ask you to read it through before signing.'

Lucy Brown

'All of you, take a seat,' Andy said. 'This won't take long. Mark's at the desk.'

Carys wondered why they were called into the office without Mark being included. She was hoping this wasn't about mistakes or a passenger complaint.

The chief explained what happened just after midnight and what Noah had experienced, leaving Carys wishing this had simply been a reprimand instead of such a tragedy. Poor Noah!

'We assume Noah Darcy was the only eye-witness apart from the man who remained onboard after the incident. This morning he gave a statement to the police.

'I would ask that none of you mention the matter either to him or anyone else.'

He looked steadily at each of them in turn.

'There were passengers still around, of course, though most were enjoying the midnight buffet. So the least said about

71

this incident the better.'

His team nodded and murmured agreement.

Carys raised her hand. Andy nodded at her.

'I'm wondering whether this other man is being held for questioning? Are we allowed to know his name?

'Everyone talks about how fast rumours spread on board so it would be good for us to know all the facts even if we're forbidden to discuss the matter.'

Andy gave her an appraising look.

'Unfortunately we've no idea who these two men were. A search-and-rescue operation is in motion but it's unlikely the unfortunate passenger will be located.

'We will, of course, be making a thorough check of all crew and passenger cabins. If the missing man was travelling with his wife or a friend I assume his sudden disappearance will cause questions.'

He checked his watch.

'Now you know as much as I do. If anyone arrives at the desk to report anything

72

unusual please bring it to my attention, no matter how trivial it seems.'

The three colleagues, having exchanged a few words with Mark, who was going off duty, began their shift.

Carys was typing names of passengers joining an excursion to the first tropical island they were due to visit after leaving Marquisa.

She looked up as someone arrived at the desk. Carys greeted her with a smile.

'Good morning, madam. How may I help you?'

The woman seemed agitated. She rested both hands on the counter and twisted her fingers together.

'It might be nothing, of course, but the friend I was due to have breakfast with in the Lilac Dining-room hasn't turned up. His name's Martin Cooper.'

'I see. Could your friend have overslept, do you think?' Carys was determined to explore all possibilities.

The woman fidgeted with her rings.

'He could have, I suppose. It's just that we met yesterday and sat next to each other for lunch and dinner and I couldn't help hoping . . .

'You know, we got on so well and it was Martin's idea to meet for breakfast today, then keep each other company on the Marquisa sightseeing trip.'

Carys consulted the handover sheet.

'May I ask your name, please?'

'I'm Lucy Brown.'

Carys frowned.

'I'm so sorry, Mrs Brown, there are no messages for you. Are there friends with whom Mr Cooper might be? Maybe he's lost track of time.'

Lucy shook her head.

'I'm a widow, travelling alone, and Martin told me he was on his own, too.

'We hit it off right away when we met at the creative-writing class yesterday morning and I must admit I've enjoyed his company.'

'Look, I'm sure there has to be some simple explanation. I'll need to look up Mr Cooper's cabin number and ask a steward to call.

'If he isn't there we could make an

announcement asking him to come to Reception.'

Lucy gasped.

'Oh, goodness, please don't do that! We've known each other such a short while and I wouldn't want him thinking I was chasing him.

'You know what they say about predatory widows taking cruises!'

Carys smiled.

'I'm sure he wouldn't think any such thing, but of course I won't put a call out if you don't want me to. Have you eaten breakfast yet?'

'Yes, I have. I thought I had better start without him. What do you think I should do now?'

'If I were you I would go ashore as planned. If Mr Cooper goes into breakfast and wonders where you've got to he'll probably come to the desk to see if you've left a message.'

Carys knew she that she needed to be tactful.

'Does he happen to know your cabin number? If so he might have pushed a note under your door by now.'

Lucy Brown reddened.

'Neither of us thought to exchange that kind of information, though now I wish we had.'

She looked thoughtful.

'OK, thank you for your help. I just can't help worrying he might have had some kind of accident or been taken poorly in the night.'

Carys nodded.

'I'll make enquiries but let's hope there's some simple explanation.'

As the woman walked away, Carys wished she herself didn't have such a worrying feeling about this man's absence.

If only Mr Cooper would arrive at the desk and ask if a passenger called Lucy Brown had left him a message.

A Nightmare

Noah knew how quickly news travelled on a ship but he was still surprised at how many people knew of his unfortunate experience the night before.

He needed to talk and there was only one person he wanted to confide in.

The young lady in question might not, of course, feel the same about him. But he knew you never achieved anything if you weren't prepared to take risks.

He decided to call at Reception and see if Carys could spare time from her busy schedule. He found her at the desk.

'Hi.' She smiled up at him. 'No trip to Marquisa for you? Oh, gosh, I'm so sorry, Noah! How thoughtless of me!'

He smiled.

'It's all right. Life must go on, and it's not as though I haven't visited the city before.

'I've been thinking about you, Carys, and I wonder whether you'd like to meet up for a coffee some time.'

'I'd love to, Noah. I was so sorry to hear about your ordeal. It must have been distressing, witnessing what you did.'

He nodded.

'It feels like a nightmare and one I'll never forget. I don't want to bring you down but having someone sympathetic to talk to would be amazing.'

'I'm due an hour's break at four. Would that suit you?'

'Perfect. How about the crew bar? It's not generally too crowded at that time.'

'Yes, especially today with so many crew members having gone ashore.'

He straightened.

'I'd better not hang about. See you in about twenty minutes.'

Noah decided to go straight to the bar and find a quiet corner. He knew he should be resting, having a show to do later on, but he'd cope. He always did.

The problem was he kept wondering whether the man involved in that horrific fall had identified him when he'd glanced up. The illuminated veranda against the ship's dark hulk surely would have highlighted anyone standing there.

Noah wasn't stupid. He knew his face was well-known, even if Carys hadn't had a clue who was fixing her shoe that first day.

If he really was the only other eye witness to what led to such a tragedy, might he himself now be in danger from that unknown passenger?

Fearful

'Have I kept you waiting?'

'Not at all.' Noah rose and pulled out a chair and Carys sank into it.

'Noah, you can tell me as much as you want. I won't breathe a word to anyone.'

'Why don't we order something to eat? Then I'd appreciate sharing my thoughts.'

'Of course.'

She wondered how she could possibly help but recognised something in him that touched her heart. If he wanted to confide in her didn't that tell her something?

He went to the bar to place their order of toasted, buttered teacakes and coffee. Carys watched him weave his way through the tables, stopping to say hello to two girls seated near the counter. They weren't in uniform so it seemed likely they were entertainers.

When he returned he sat opposite her, took off his spectacles and put them on the table. Only then did he gaze at her with the smile every single one of his fans felt was meant only for them.

Anything Carys knew about Noah came from her colleagues. Her previous job, in the hotel conference business, had gobbled up her life, making her feel she'd lost herself as a person.

Here on the cruise ship her rôle was focused on ensuring the passengers enjoyed their stay aboard *The Golden Goddess*. She loved working in this holiday atmosphere so last night's events had hit her hard.

'I know we mustn't go into details but I'm so very sorry you got involved.'

'Who would have thought something like this could happen? I'm not ashamed to admit I'm shaken up.'

'That doesn't surprise me,' Carys said. 'I don't suppose you'd contemplate letting your understudy go on this evening?'

'Correct. I'll feel better once I'm on stage. All that matters then is to convince the audience I really am a lonely cowboy, or pining for a girl who's engaged to be married to somebody else!'

'Or you're an angel in black leather come down to earth to help someone in need?'

He chuckled.

'Yes! Have you seen the show?'

She knew he was teasing. He was well aware she had had no idea how famous he was that day he'd almost fallen over her. Swiftly she pulled herself together.

'My last job didn't allow time for a personal life. I don't suppose I'll see you all perform some of the scenes on this trip?'

'No way. The show's still far too new. Tonight we're giving them 'Carousel' and I'm playing Billy, the bad boy.' He grinned. 'You don't have to pretend you know that show, either.'

'As it happens I do! My mum took me to see the film when I was about twelve.'

'Gordon MacRae and Shirley Jones.' He nodded. 'Sublime. Great choice, Carys's mum!'

'She'd adore you,' Carys blurted out. 'She'd be asking all kinds of questions about show business and where you trained.'

Suddenly she couldn't believe she'd talked about her mother meeting Noah Darcy. He must now think she had a massive crush on him!

She cringed, not knowing where to look and wondering why she kept putting her foot in it.

Luckily their food and drinks arrived. Both were peckish so they ate in silence until Noah sipped his coffee and looked across at her.

'Carys, do you mind if I ask you something?'

'That's my job,' she said lightly.

'To be honest, yesterday I'd wondered about asking whether you fancied going into the city with me today.

'I didn't get around to it and, of course, my midnight adventure put paid to going ashore today.

'I opted to stay on board but I do hope to go ashore at Porto Claro. I've been wishing I could spend time with you without pouring out my troubles.'

'I enjoy your company, Noah. You don't need to entertain me and whatever you say will go no further.'

'Thank you. I'm so glad Fate threw you into my path.'

He was probably only being polite.

'Me and my suitcase, you mean!' Her smile faded as she saw the expression on his face.

His brown eyes weren't sparkling with fun now. What she saw in them took her breath away. She felt sure he wasn't acting.

'Yes, brought together by a snapped-off heel and a suitcase. I wonder if that would make a good song!'

Carys chuckled, relieved he'd broken the tension.

'Doubt it. What did you want to say?'

'It's just that, while those two guys were arguing, I was standing on the veranda which must have made me clearly visible from below.

'They were too busy slinging insults until that final moment when the man accusing the other one of fraud lunged at the big man just as the ship pitched. The impetus sent the smaller man straight over the rail.'

Noah shuddered and took another swallow of coffee.

'That's how I described it to the detective. My concern is that the passenger left on deck appeared to look up at me as the ship pitched. Now do you understand what's bugging me?'

Carys stared at him.

'I do but I'm not sure how well he'd have been able to see you from the lower deck. Also he'd have been furious, determined not to let his accuser get away with anything and in no condition to realise he was looking at Noah Darcy, West-End star!'

Noah considered.

'I hope you're right.' He placed his cutlery together. 'But what if you're not? The moment he sees me again, whether in one of the restaurants or if he watches my show, he could realise he's looking at the only person on board who witnessed an incident that could make life very

85

difficult for him if I recognise him and tell the authorities!'

She bit her lip.

'If he was challenged he'd probably insist he was nowhere near that part of the deck at the time. You can't make a positive identification, can you?'

'I don't think so. The man was broad-shouldered and much taller than the poor bloke who was drowned.' He paused. 'At least, we assume he drowned.

'The big fellow's voice was deep. At one point he laughed out loud and it was a really distinctive sound. I might well recognise that laugh if I heard it again.

'But there are two thousand passengers on board, aren't there?'

'Almost, yes. Did you notice the man's hair colour? Was he clean-shaven?'

Carys's heart thumped a little faster. Poor Noah must have already given all this information to the Marquisa police detective.

He shrugged.

'Difficult to say. His hair seemed dark and he might have had the beginnings of a beard. I couldn't be of much help to the detective when he asked for a description.

'I wonder if he'd been injured during the struggle and got a black eye or a scratch.'

Noah sighed.

'It might sound selfish but I hope whoever it was couldn't see me properly when he looked up.'

Just Friends

Carys returned to work feeling she'd got to know Noah a lot better. He was such easy company and didn't seem to care whether or not she was one of his fans.

He had even appeared embarrassed when she told him how much she enjoyed hearing him sing when she'd slipped into the music lounge the night before.

She hoped he'd listened when she reassured him. She had also offered to report his qualms to her boss and suggest standing on the veranda late in the evening while someone stood on the deck below, to discover whether her face was recognisable.

Carys knocked on Andy's door as soon as the desk was quiet. Her boss was on the phone but he waved at her to sit down.

Moments later he replaced the receiver.

'Nothing's wrong, I hope? You seem to be settling in well, Carys.'

'I'm loving it, thanks. I came to say

I've been taking my break with Noah Darcy.'

Andy leaned back in his chair, balancing a pencil between his two forefingers.

'Ah. So, how many heartbroken female passengers will be visiting Sick Bay, do you think? Should I warn the chief nurse?'

Carys couldn't help laughing.

'Noah and I are just friends.' She explained how they'd first met. 'I hadn't realised how quickly friendships can begin on a ship. It's like entering a different world, isn't it?'

'It is. I know you and Tina met while you were waiting to board and I'm pleased you two have hit it off. She told me she'd informed you of our relationship. Tina doesn't make friends easily, you know.'

'I recognise that feeling from my last job.' Carys made a wry face.

'I hope you both find time to meet now and then. Now, what's on your mind?'

She outlined what Noah had confided and explained he was happy for her to seek Andy's advice. She also related the suggestion she'd made to help Noah feel less concerned about being recognised.

Andy shook his head.

'Here's the thing. If we establish that someone below can clearly see who's standing on the veranda won't that make Noah even more concerned?'

He rose and paced across the room with his hands clasped behind his back.

'I'm inclined to leave things be. It would be difficult to recreate that incident accurately given the weather conditions last night. Not to mention the height difference between you and Mr Heartthrob!'

He gave her a quizzical look. Carys wondered if she'd ever become too sophisticated to blush.

'I was hardly aware of his existence before I arrived at Southampton Docks!'

'Really?' Andy sat back down. 'Noah must find that extremely refreshing. I imagine he values the company of someone who isn't drooling while sitting opposite him.'

'I certainly enjoy his company,' Carys said primly.

Now, that really was an understatement!

'Hmm. I have a lot of time for that young man,' Andy said. 'He's got his head screwed on — always an advantage when you're in the business he's in.

'But this is your first cruise with us, Carys, and I can't help hoping your friendship doesn't develop into a shipboard romance. Although I'm a fine one to talk!'

'I'm not going to do anything daft, Andy. I enjoy being part of your team and so far, fingers crossed, I haven't suffered from seasickness.'

'Be thankful for stabilisers. Now, let's think. What can we do to convince our star performer he's not in grave danger?'

'Any News?'

Passengers were returning to the ship and Carys faced a problem. Unless her friend, Martin, had turned up Lucy Brown would be back to enquire about him.

Mr Cooper's steward had reported nothing unusual. The passenger was tidy in his habits and his clothes were all put away, except for his pyjamas which lay on the bed, neatly folded.

The bed itself looked as though it hadn't been slept in. Nobody by that name had visited the medical centre.

She reported her concerns to Andy.

'What if he's the man who fell overboard? What do I say to Mrs Brown when she asks if we've located her friend? She's sure to come to the desk before she returns to her cabin.'

Andy rubbed his chin.

'We need to tread carefully. I've done this job for a while now and I know there are passengers of both sex who look upon a cruise as an opportunity to find romance.'

'You mean he could have just given the poor woman the heave-ho? Charmed some other unsuspecting lady and, while Lucy was in Marquisa, spent the day with his new romance? That would be quick work!'

'I could be wrong but we daren't commit ourselves until we find him.'

Andy checked his watch.

'When Mrs Brown turns up I know you'll be tactful. Firstly, tell her we're doing our best to locate him but that, if he's decided to discontinue their friendship, well . . .'

'I'll do my best. In case I've gone off duty when she arrives I'll make sure Suzanne knows the score.'

'Excellent. Are you going to the show tonight?'

'All being well, yes.'

'That's good. You should try to relax, Carys. This is a difficult situation with too many loose threads for my liking.

'I'll make sure each head waiter knows

we're anxious to establish Mr Cooper's whereabouts. If he doesn't turn up for dinner I'll have his cabin steward make inquiries among his colleagues.

'We should know something by tomorrow morning at the latest.'

'I'd love to be proved wrong. Thanks, Andy. I'll try to forget everything and enjoy the show.'

She let herself out and heard Suzanne call her name.

'Carys, Mrs Brown would like a word.'

'Thanks, Suzanne.'

She approached the counter.

'Hello! How was Marquisa?'

'Great, thanks. I joined up with two ladies travelling together and we made the most of our time. It's a very elegant city.'

Lucy lowered her voice.

'Any news of Martin? I kept an eye out for him when we were disembarking and then coming back on board just now.'

Carys relayed the information as tactfully and calmly as possible.

Lucy nodded.

'I did wonder whether he'd got cold feet about our getting together.' She shrugged. 'OK. It was nice while it lasted. I just wouldn't have thought he could be so discourteous after being such good company the day before.'

She sighed.

'Anyway, I'm grateful for your help.'

'That's why I'm here. Enjoy your evening.'

Watching Lucy walk away Carys wondered what would happen next. If Martin Cooper was still on board it seemed unlikely he'd miss dinner after having paid beforehand for his cruise holiday.

If he didn't make an appearance could they really assume he'd gone to Davy Jones's Locker?

A Deep Voice

Though Carys remembered little of the film she'd seen years before with her mother she was delighted to watch the company perform scenes from 'Carousel'.

The theatre was packed but she could see well from her corner and was glad to have something to take her mind off the current situation.

Some of the scenes were extremely emotional and Noah's performance surprised her with its intensity.

He was blessed not only with a super voice but with being a good actor, too.

Carys felt sure, once he returned to London, he'd have no trouble landing another leading rôle.

After rapturous applause and several curtain calls the audience was leaving.

Carys was amused to note that several passengers she'd dealt with at the desk only gave her a glance, or a polite smile and nod. Dressed in a fuchsia-pink trouser suit with her hair loose on her shoulders she probably shouldn't expect to be recognised.

Rupert and Summer Maitland were outside the theatre entrance, chatting with another couple, as Carys passed.

She glanced at Summer but wouldn't have dreamed of interrupting her conversation had Summer not called to her.

'I almost didn't recognise you in your gorgeous outfit, darling. How did you enjoy the show?'

'I loved it but the theme is quite dark in places, isn't it? I probably didn't appreciate how much when I saw the film as a twelve-year-old.'

'That's true. I was saying to Rupert and our friends how fortunate it is that Noah is so versatile. Billy is very different from his last rôle. Did you see 'Angel In Black Leather'?'

'Sadly, no. Maybe I can catch it once it goes on tour — work permitting, of course.'

Summer tossed her hair back.

'Do try, it's fabulous. Well, I mustn't

keep you, darling. I'm sure you have more exciting things to do in your off-duty time than be nice to passengers!'

'It's always a pleasure to talk to you, Mrs Maitland.' Carys smiled at her.

Rupert said goodnight to the other couple then turned. He nodded.

'Good evening. It's, um, Carys, isn't it? Hardly recognised you wearing civvies,' the burly businessman said.

She decided Mr Maitland didn't have the look of a man entirely relaxed and enjoying his evening. He kept casting quick glances around the people who stood chatting nearby.

The man towered over both his wife and Carys and was probably well into his fifties but his dark hair was only slightly tinged with grey.

He was obviously using this time at sea to grow a beard as dark stubble shadowing his cheeks and chin.

This made her recollect the description Noah had given and, as someone nearby called Rupert by name, he turned around and she heard him his deep voice booming in answer.

Carys said goodnight to Summer and headed for her cabin.

She longed to share her suspicions with Noah but it wouldn't be fair to hang around, hoping to see him, after the eventful 24 hours he'd had.

Nevertheless she would find it difficult to quieten her thoughts ready for sleep tonight.

Could Rupert Maitland be the mystery man whom Noah had seen arguing with the missing passenger?

Amateur Detectives

Noah woke a little later than usual. He liked to go for a jog first thing and had a favourite route.

He pulled on jogging pants and sweat-shirt, pushed his feet into trainers and was about to leave his cabin when he saw a small envelope lying on the carpet.

He tore open the envelope, surprised to find a handwritten letter inside.

Dear Noah,

I have a possible actor in mind for the character we were discussing. I'm looking forward to seeing your face when I tell you.

You may not know this man but I'll explain why I think he fits the bill when we meet. If you have time, please call at the desk today or tomorrow. We can talk about the next shore excursion and I'll slip the name into our conversation.

Congratulations on a fantastic show last night! I understand now why Frank Sinatra thought Billy Bigelow was the best-ever rôle for a male singer in musical theatre.

Some of my mum's knowledge of musicals is coming back to me. I hope you're impressed!

You seemed to combine Billy's vulnerability with his arrogance and get the audience on your side — certainly the women. Maybe we all secretly admire a bad boy?

Hope to see you soon,
Carys.

Noah folded the note and buried it beneath the underwear in his top drawer.

He wasn't suspicious by nature but, since becoming well-known for his musical theatre performances, he took care where he stored anything of a personal nature.

He got on well with his cabin steward and Carys, clever girl, hadn't given any impression she was writing about anything more serious than a casting suggestion.

Although it was a mild morning he

pulled his hood over his head once he got outside in an effort to be as unobtrusive as possible.

Usually this tactic worked. He'd also learned it was best to visit the well-equipped gym while most passengers were enjoying their lunch.

There was so much he wanted to ask Carys. Different scenarios entered his head as he completed two circuits of the deck.

If he couldn't confirm that her suspect was the man he saw then he would need to hear the man speak.

He might have to do some careful shadowing but then, wouldn't that prove to be unwise if the suspect suddenly recognised him?

Once showered and dressed in his usual jeans and T-shirt, ready for rehearsal, he headed towards breakfast.

After his meal Noah couldn't wait to find Carys, telling himself she was his best way of extricating himself from the hole he occupied.

He saw her as he approached

Reception, catching his breath as he watched her chuckle at a remark made by the person she was helping.

Still, alarm bells rang in his head. He'd joined this cruise to disappear from London's Theatreland for several weeks. The last thing he should do was become involved with another girl, no matter how lovely and sweet she might be.

It was far better to consider Carys as a friend and part of an amateur detective partnership.

He put on his professional face as two women approached, probably mother and daughter, wanting to tell him how much they enjoyed the previous night's show.

He spent a couple of minutes chatting, then turned to see Carys had stepped back from the desk.

Noah made his apologies to the two passengers and headed towards her.

'Good morning.'

She turned round and on seeing him her face lit up. Noah's heart almost tripped over itself and, lost in the moment, he forgot all thoughts of warning bells and common-sense.

But he'd be stupid to ignore the potential danger he might be facing. Carys was the only person he could trust enough to confide his fears in right now.

Whatever else was between them must take a back seat until this situation was resolved.

'Hi.' He smiled at her. 'Thanks for your note. I'm intrigued but, to be honest, I'm not sure how we deal with this.

'I think I must be guided by you.'

She smiled.

'Obviously I've said nothing yet to Andy but he wanted me to reassure you that you're not in any danger from this unknown passenger.

'He agreed with me that it was highly unlikely the man recognised you.'

'I wish I could believe that!' Noah ran his hand through his hair. 'Why do you and Andy think that?'

'You're remembering the incident as an observer. The man in question was in the midst of it and had a lot on his mind.

'You say you saw him glance upwards but the motion of the ship caused him to lose his balance. Both Andy and I doubt you were as noticeable as you think you were.'

Carys checked no-one was nearby before leaning across the counter.

'Rupert Maitland fits the description you gave,' she whispered. 'Do you know who I mean?'

Noah pulled off his glasses and rubbed the bridge of his nose.

'I don't think so. Wait. Do you mean Summer's husband?'

'That's right. I doubt you'd find anyone among the passengers who's larger than he is. Also I noticed him go out on deck after he saw his wife into the elevator.'

Noah looked behind him.

'I'd better let you do your job. Can you spare half an hour this afternoon?'

'I'm dining in the Orchid Restaurant tonight — Andy's orders. Shall we meet on deck at four o'clock, outside the door over to starboard?' She nodded to her right.

'See you then. And, Carys, thank you.'

He strode off, leaving her with a bunch of eager passengers seeking advice on places to visit when going ashore at Porto Claro.

Lost Property

A tall burly figure loomed before the desk. Carys drew herself up to her full height.

'Good morning, sir. I hope all's going well for you and your wife.'

Could the man towering over her really be the crooked boss who'd been confronted by his former employee?

She tried to shut out the image of a body plummeting through the air and disappearing into the depths of the ocean.

Her hands were trembling and Rupert seemed to notice. She clasped them behind her back.

'Everything's fine. I'd like to discuss my wife's birthday. It is in a few days' time.'

Was the purser's team aware of this? It was news to her.

'If we've been informed by your office, Mr Maitland, there will be a birthday bouquet delivered to your suite on the morning of Mrs Maitland's special day.'

She couldn't help wondering whether he had recognised Noah in the show last night. Chills ran down her back at the thought of what a desperate man might do to keep himself in the clear.

Rupert Maitland looked doubtful.

'My PA is extremely efficient but things were hectic before I left the office. It would be good to know whether Summer's birthday is logged or not.

'I want to arrange a special dinner in our suite with half-a-dozen guests joining us. Understand I intend this as a surprise and I expect you all to keep it from her.

'The dinner must take place on the evening of Wednesday, December 22.' Carys wrote the date on her notepad.

The liner would have left the island of Jarnesia and be heading for the Caribbean resort of White Keys.

'We have celebration menus designed for such an occasion. You can take a look now or would you prefer that your cabin steward brings you a menu some time when your wife is otherwise engaged?'

'Hmm. She has taken to attending the creative-writing sessions with that author fellow, Willoughby Franks.'

'I'm glad Mrs Maitland's enjoying her sessions.' Carys smiled.

'Really can't see the point,' he grumbled. 'Summer's a top journalist — she can probably teach this chap a thing or two!'

Carys decided it was best to humour him and he seemed pleased his weak joke had gone down well.

How can you behave as though nothing's happened, she wondered, then told herself not to jump to conclusions. Rupert Maitland wasn't the only tall, dark, broad-shouldered man on board.

He was looking at her.

'In case Summer changes her mind about attending I'll take a quick look now, then talk to you after I plan the day and finalise the guest list.'

Carys reached beneath the desk for a gilt-embossed leather folder.

'Take your time, Mr Maitland.

Meanwhile I'll deal with this gentleman, if that's all right.'

Rupert shifted his position out of the way of the waiting passenger. A quick glance showed Carys that he was fingering his cheek.

Her breath caught in her throat. That cut on his right cheek looked like a recent injury judging by the dried blood.

Had he been injured while struggling with the missing passenger?

Out of the corner of her eye she saw him put the leather folder on the counter.

'Sorry, I just remembered I've promised to meet someone. I'll call back later.'

He turned and went on his way, making Carys speculate whether a guilty conscience was causing his forgetfulness.

She dealt with more queries then noticed one of the cleaners waiting for her to be free. She read his name badge.

'Is everything all right, Mike? Did you want to speak to the chief?'

'I need to hand something in. A child spilled lemonade out on deck and I got a call to clear up the mess.'

He held out his right hand, palm upwards.

Carys peered at what lay there.

'A tie pin! It looks valuable, doesn't it? Where exactly did you find it, Mike?'

'A few yards up from the starboard entrance. My guess is it got lodged between planks and my brushing freed it.'

He moved away, leaving Carys staring down at her palm where she held someone's missing treasure.

If this tie pin really was solid gold, and if the gleaming teardrop pearl in the centre of the bar was a genuine one, then the person who owned it would surely call to enquire whether it had been found.

Unless — her mind was racing — unless Mike had found it in the exact place Noah witnessed the argument the other night.

What if the big man had lost the pin while struggling with his attacker?

A False Name

Noah was waiting on deck when Carys arrived. He admired the way she carried herself.

'Do you fancy walking for a bit?'

'Good idea. I could do with the fresh air.'

He balled his fists at his sides, fighting the urge to reach for her hand.

'Have you ever taken ballet lessons?'

'When I was a little kid, yes. What makes you ask?'

'Your deportment's really good, is all.'

'Thank you. Sadly Dad changed jobs when I was nine and after we moved ballet lessons got forgotten.'

'That's a pity. You might have ended up as a professional dancer! Our paths could have crossed in the West End.'

'We're here to discuss your situation,' she reminded him.

He shoved his hands in his pockets.

'I know, but it shouldn't always be about me. Learning about you is important. I like to imagine that little girl, dressed up as a sunflower, dancing around the village hall.'

Carys giggled.

'As far as I recall it was a church hall. But let me tell you my latest findings.'

She described how she'd noticed a mark on Rupert's cheek.

'I need to see this fellow for myself,' Noah decided. 'Summer has asked me for an exclusive interview but she said Rupert won't be around.

'If she does a good job, and I imagine she will, my agent will be pleased and hopefully I'll win back some of the fans I lost by — according to them — deserting both Georgie and my rôle in the show.'

Some of Carys's colleagues had told her about Noah's split from his former girlfriend. She changed the subject.

'The other thing I have to tell you might turn out to be important evidence.'

She explained how a cleaner had found a tie pin just where Rupert and his former employee had played out their drama.

Noah whistled softly.

'Crikey! What did you do with it?'

'We have a drawer where we keep any small objects handed in. Only the team knows where the key to that drawer is kept.

'But if that tie pin does belong to Rupert do you think he'd dare report its loss if it fell off while he was struggling with the missing man?'

Noah nodded.

'He could have walked along that same bit of deck every day, couldn't he?'

'True, but if that tie pin's as expensive as it appears to be, and he genuinely lost it when taking his daily walk, why not come to Reception and ask if it's been found?

'Anyway, surely he'd only wear it for a formal occasion. I remember he was wearing evening dress the night he watched your show.'

The breeze lifted Carys's hair so it blew around her face. Noah, forgetting about detection theories, stopped walking and smoothed her hair from her eyes.

He bent and kissed the side of her mouth.

'Oh, my goodness!'

'I'm sorry, Carys. That was out of order.'

'Don't apologise. I didn't mean I didn't enjoy it.'

She stood looking at him and he longed to kiss her again but he became aware of a group of people coming their way.

'Let's keep walking.'

'OK. I'd really love to know whether that pin belongs to Rupert or not,' Carys told him. 'He was definitely wearing a dinner jacket the night you performed. It's not hard to imagine the pin falling out if he and the other man were brawling.'

'Good point. Go on.'

They were nearing a secluded bench. Noah understood the importance of Carys's conclusions but all he could think of was whether he dared kiss her again while there was nobody else around.

'What if I ask him outright whether

he's lost a tie pin?' she mused. 'Say one's been handed in and it's so stylish and valuable that I thought it was worth checking to see whether he'd lost it.'

Noah frowned.

'If he's on the defensive he could bluster and tell you he has several so he'd have to check. He'd have to decide how much value he places upon that tie pin.

'If he's worried by evidence linking him to the accident he might pretend it's not his.'

'I think,' Carys responded, 'it would be even more interesting to catch him with Summer there. More chance of his guard being down.

'But you don't think Rupert will be around when you visit their suite?'

'Not according to Summer. Even if he's there I daren't say anything. I've never seen him up close but I do remember the big man's deep voice.

'I clearly heard him address the newcomer as Simon.'

Carys stopped walking.

'Simon! Are you certain it was Simon?'

'Yes. I told the detective that. Didn't I mention it?'

'No. Noah, Simon is the name of the person Rupert asked about on the second day of the cruise! He came to me and asked if I could check whether someone called Simon Waters was on the passenger list.

'I shouldn't be telling you that but we have to trust each other if we're going to get to the bottom of this business.'

Noah nodded.

'You know I won't say a word to anyone. Was he? On the list, I mean.'

'No. Andy checked the crew list, too. There's no-one of that name on board.'

She looked at him and he gasped.

'That means, whoever Simon was booked his passage under a false name! Different passport and papers.'

'Top marks, Sherlock.'

Noah chuckled. He loved her teasing him.

She was gazing at the sky.

'I think that's a pelican up there. I've never seen one actually flying before.'

117

She pointed and he followed her gaze.

'All that sky and sea. I imagine you'll see lots of wild life, working on cruise ships. And I don't mean the passengers!'

Carys didn't laugh. She was thinking about Lucy Brown and how she knew the missing man as Martin Cooper.

Private Eye

They carried on walking. Noah turned to Carys.

'I should tell you I have a friend who runs a private detective agency in London. We were at school together in Northampton but lost touch after I went to drama college and Luke joined the police force.'

'Two very different career paths!'

'Yes. I used to hear how he was doing over the years but we never met until one day I walked into a steak house in Covent Garden and Luke was there.

'It was as if we'd never been separated. He told me he'd left the police force and started a private detective agency.

'Luke's a great bloke and I know, if I contact him, he'll do his best to dig into Maitland's company affairs.'

Carys stopped walking. The ship chose that moment to pitch a little and Noah reached out, pulling her into his arms.

He looked down at her, breathing in

the fresh, lemony scent of her hair and knowing he need only bend his head a little and he could kiss her. But was he rushing her?

She solved his problem by pulling away gently.

'That's the second time I've needed to thank you for saving me from disaster. I wonder how long it'll take for me to gain my sea legs!'

Noah regretted his missed opportunity but the moment was gone. It would seem clumsy to steal a kiss now.

'You'll be fine,' he said. 'What do you think? Shall I get my mate to take me on as a client?'

They sat down together, gazing out to sea. The water was choppy but not excessively so.

The sky was a radiant cornflower blue and Noah suddenly felt more optimistic.

Carys turned to him.

'How much information would you need to supply? It would be more than my job was worth if I passed any confidential details to you, like the name of

Rupert's company or his home address.'

'Don't worry. I heard his company name mentioned but I get the impression Rupert Maitland is wealthy enough for Luke to know how to pin him down.

'He'll access company records and check for any fraudulent activity.'

'Let me get this straight,' she said. 'It's unlikely we can prove Rupert was to blame for the accident. If you get a look at him and feel sure he's the man you saw it'll still be your word against his.

'He'd get a top barrister to defend him if it came to the crunch, anyway. It was night time; the weather wasn't brilliant; you weren't close enough to see clearly, blah, blah, blah.'

She had a sudden thought.

'Were you wearing your specs, Noah?'

'Yes, I was. But if Rupert needed an alibi he'd have to ask his wife to lie to vouch for him being with her. My statement records the time I went on to the veranda.

'Wow, talking it through with you has helped me remember little details that could be very important.'

Carys stared at him.

'Likewise! When I noticed him help Summer into the elevator, then go on deck, I glanced at the clock. It was almost midnight.'

'You'd swear to that?'

'I would.' She glanced at her watch. 'I'd better get back. I need to freshen up ready for later.'

'I hope you enjoy eating with the posh people!'

'I'll probably feel as if I should be on my best behaviour but I'm sure they're perfectly nice and friendly.'

She hesitated.

'Noah, are you certain you want to go to such trouble? Get a private detective involved?

'I truly think Rupert hasn't a clue anyone witnessed that argument. I wouldn't mind betting he thinks he's in the clear.'

Noah shrugged, unhappy.

'From my point of view I hope you're right but it's not just about me. No way should he get away with fraud, let alone be the cause of a man losing his life.

'I got the impression the detective I spoke to was more interested in the disappearance of the man who fell overboard rather than what led up to it.

'Crime at sea — if we are talking about crime here — is difficult to deal with if there's no body nor any way of proving or disproving Simon Waters was pushed overboard.' He frowned. 'It looked like an unfortunate accident to me but some might suggest it was a case of manslaughter.'

'You want to see justice done, though?'

'Yes.'

'Then somehow,' Carys told him, 'we have to find a way of proving Rupert Maitland is the mystery man.'

Odious Man

'I'd like brunch served in our suite at ten o'clock on the day,' Rupert Maitland said. 'Chilled fresh orange juice and champagne, croissants, scrambled eggs and smoked salmon.'

'Yes, sir.' Carys was making notes.

'Book Summer in at the beauty salon that afternoon, say at three o'clock so she has time for a siesta beforehand.'

'I'll inform the manageress Mrs Maitland will probably require the full package. The staff have had the pleasure of caring for her before and I know they'll do all they can to accommodate her wishes.'

He was positively beaming! Odious man. Summer had no idea her husband was, according to his former company secretary, a fraudster with no conscience.

To think that Carys had told her colleague, Suzanne, how much Mrs Maitland must love her husband. It was horrible to imagine how any wife would feel when discovering what evil deeds the husband she loved and trusted was capable of.

She thought of Noah and that made her feel better. If only his private investigator pal could get to the bottom of the allegations against Rupert.

So far there had been no news of a body found washed up on some lonely shore, and certainly nobody found alive, clinging to a piece of driftwood.

It was sinister that Rupert hadn't raised the alarm. That was surely indicative of his guilt! He'd probably been scuttling back to his suite while Noah sought help.

She collected her thoughts, seeing Rupert look at her enquiringly.

'So sorry, I was just reminding myself to order corsages for the four ladies. The timing for the dinner is perfect as we'll still be in White Keys Harbour and our florist will have her pick of exotic blooms.'

He beamed again.

'Good girl for thinking about flowers.

My wife adores orchids, if that's any help.'

'I'm sure it will be, sir. Maybe neutral shades as we don't know what colour dresses your lady guests will be wearing.'

'My wife will be in midnight blue. Tina, our stewardess, is looking after the dress as it's a birthday gift.'

'I'll add that to the florist's information.'

'Do you know, um, Carys, I told you right at the beginning how I thought you'd do well in your new post. I do enjoy being proved right.'

This was irritating. She wanted to slap him and have him clapped in irons. Or make him walk the plank!

She contemplated asking how he got that nasty nick on his cheek but thought better of it. If only she could obtain a photograph!

The conversation moved to the dinner menu. Salad, scallops, scampi, lobster . . . a refreshing sorbet before the main course of Beef Wellington with fresh vegetables.

Next Rupert specified his preference

for the cheeseboard to be served, French style, before the dessert, which must be a choice between orange chocolate fondue and Black Forest gâteau.

After Rupert was sure he'd thought of everything, including the wine, he went away, having informed Carys he anticipated winning a few pennies from his card school chums.

'I bet you are. You probably cheat, anyway!' she muttered to his retreating form.

The more she saw of this man the more she hoped he would receive his comeuppance before too much longer.

The Interview

It was clear Summer Maitland was a big fan of musical theatre and had seen many more shows than Noah. She told him, teasing, that he'd catch up when he got to be as old as she was.

They were served cold drinks and nibbles in the sitting-room and chatted together comfortably until Summer suggested they sit outside for his interview.

They moved to the suite's private balcony. The air was balmy, the sea calm and the sun shining.

Noah knew that the fresh air and sunshine were doing more for him than any vitamin pills could but he was aware that he needed to be careful not to get a suntan.

'So, tell me what's next for Noah Darcy,' Summer invited.

'My agent's pushing me either to join a new UK tour or to take another West End rôle. There are a couple of good ones coming up in shows that have done well on Broadway.'

He hesitated.

'There's another option that I prefer to keep under my hat for now.'

'Darling, you're such a spoilsport! This is just the kind of thing I'm after.' She pouted.

'Sorry, Summer, but the current lead rôle is played by someone who's going into a TV soap opera after Christmas.

'I know you'll understand I wouldn't want to steal his thunder, especially as he's a good friend.'

She smiled.

'I respect your professionalism. Would you ever consider joining one of the soaps?'

'Me? Heavens, no. I enjoy singing too much to do that.'

'Never say never, darling. You might receive an offer too good to refuse. You'd certainly cause a huge rise in viewing figures.'

He chuckled.

'I'm probably a better singer than I am an actor.'

'That's not what the critics say. But let's continue.'

An hour later she declared she had enough material for her feature.

'I may decide to hold it until the end of the cruise so that we can add any extras if you hear something exciting from your agent.'

'I promise you'll be the first to know.'

Noah decided this might be a good time to fish for information as the journalist's mood seemed mellow.

'I was wondering if I would meet your husband today, though you said he'd probably be playing cards.'

She pulled off her sunglasses.

'Probably best if you don't; he's a little too grumpy lately for my liking.'

'I'm sorry to hear that. Isn't he enjoying the cruise?'

She shrugged.

'He seemed fine until the night we watched you perform all those fabulous songs. I can't put my finger on it.'

'Oh, dear. I hope one of my numbers didn't upset him. Songs can bring back painful memories as well as happy ones.'

'Don't fret, darling. Rupert isn't sensitive about such things. He seemed preoccupied at breakfast next morning but I've learned not to push him for information.

'It might be to do with my birthday and that he's planning a surprise.'

She nodded as if that sorted out the matter.

Noah took off his glasses.

'I'd better make a move.'

'So soon? I've really enjoyed our chat, darling. Let's hope I can make something worth reading from it.'

'I can't imagine you producing anything that isn't fascinating.' He rose and smiled down at her. 'Enjoy the rest of your day. I can see myself out.'

'Before you go what delights do you have for us tonight? I forgot to check the daily schedule.'

'We'll be performing a medley from 'South Pacific'.'

'You'll be playing Joe Cable, the marine?'

'Yep. Another hero who bites the dust!'

'Yes, but then he sings one of my favourite songs — 'Younger Than Springtime'. I'll come to the early performance.

'If Rupert's not too tired I can be back in time for a quiet supper with him.'

Noah let himself out. It was interesting that Summer had admitting noticing a change in her husband's mood.

That couldn't be coincidence.

He decided to head for the crew bar. Suki had asked him when he'd be done with his interview and, although Noah didn't want to encourage her, it would be impolite to snub her.

Uneasy

When Noah walked by Carys was absorbed in a task so he didn't interrupt her. As always, when he saw her obviously enjoying her job, he smiled.

She gave him a happy feeling and he was pleased their amateur-detective partnership provided an excuse to meet.

He could do without the occasional uneasy feelings swamping him sometimes. When walking on deck, especially after dark, he couldn't resist turning his head in case anyone was creeping up on him.

He must be prepared to come face to face with Maitland some time, though the longer he went without doing so the less he felt it likely the tycoon would murder a fellow passenger in cold blood!

In the crew bar he saw a group of performers, including Suki. As he went up to the counter Suki joined him.

'How did your interview go?'

'Fine, thanks. We got on well but it

might take a while before the feature's published.'

He turned to the attendant waiting to serve him.

'I'd like a tuna and mayonnaise sandwich, please, and tea for one. I'll wait so you don't need to bring them over.'

Suki edged closer.

'Summer's piece will be worth waiting for, I'm sure.'

Noah felt uncomfortable. He wished Suki wouldn't stand so close.

He took his order over to the table where Suki sat beside him until the party looked like breaking up.

Steve and another lad were going for a swim. Others said they needed to catch up with their sleep.

Noah made a play of yawning.

'Wow, I should take a rest, too. Must be all that sunshine!'

He was hoping to catch another glimpse of Carys on his way back but didn't think she'd appreciate his turning up with Suki clinging to his arm.

The dancer surprised him, though.

'I'm running low on toothpaste so I'm off to the shop. See you all later.'

Noah headed for Reception but there was no sign of Carys and he didn't like to question her colleague. She could be taking a break in her cabin.

He very much hoped she'd agree to go ashore with him when the ship dropped anchor at Porto Claro.

Quizzing Tina

With Marquisa behind them and *The Golden Goddess* heading for the next port of call festive decorations began appearing in the restaurants and lounges.

Overnight, it seemed to Carys, Santa's elves had draped long strings of multi-coloured tinsel around the walls and had placed evergreen garlands all over the place.

A tall Christmas tree stood by the door of each restaurant, with smaller versions in the bars. Every tree dripped with gleaming gold and silver baubles and miniature lanterns in fruit-gum colours, together with angels dressed in white who gazed down from each tree's topmost branch.

The passengers' spirits were good, the purser's team decided. Andy had been worried about rumours spreading as people learned of the tragedy but everyone believed that the unfortunate passenger's fall was an accident.

People, therefore, although saddened and shocked, felt they needn't fear a murdering fiend creeping up behind them.

'Don't you think it's amazing how quickly word gets around on a ship?' Carys commented to Tina during a rare get-together for coffee after they were both off duty.

'Yes, also worrying. I wouldn't want to be the subject of ship's gossip!'

'It would have been difficult to keep that unfortunate passenger's disappearance completely under wraps,' Carys acknowledged.

'I agree. Andy thinks it's unlikely anyone will ever know exactly what happened. In other words, Mr Cooper took the secret with him.'

Tina shivered, picked up her cup and cradled it with both hands.

'I hope you're not regretting your decision to work on a cruise ship?'

'Not at all, though it's worrying to think someone might be walking round, knowing exactly what happened to Mr Cooper.'

'You don't believe it was an accident, then?'

Carys knew she was on shaky ground. Andy had obviously not mentioned Noah to his girlfriend and she didn't feel it was her place to tell Tina there was one eye-witness on board.

Still, Tina, being the Maitlands' stewardess, was well-placed to notice changes in Rupert's behaviour or any suspicions Summer might have.

Apparently some passengers treated their stewardess as they did their hairdresser and confided secrets they would never tell others usually.

'Tina, I'd appreciate it if you don't mention this to Andy. I'm trying to establish something for — for a friend.

'Please don't think you are obliged to answer this question but it would be helpful if you could.'

'Goodness, Carys, whatever is it?'

'Well, I was just wondering if the Maitlands are travelling with any very valuable jewellery?'

'Yes, they are. Mrs M. showed me

some of it.' Tina lowered her voice. 'She has the most beautiful emerald and diamond necklace to match her engagement ring.

'Those two items are probably the most precious. Mr Maitland is obviously head over heels in love with her.'

'I'm sure he is,' Carys murmured.

Tina shot her a quizzical look.

'Hey, you're not a jewel thief in your spare time, are you?'

'Shush, don't tell everyone!' Carys chuckled. 'No, I'm just curious. I wondered whether Mr Maitland might have another surprise up his sleeve for his wife.

'He told me about the blue dress, by the way, but rest assured I'm very good at keeping quiet.'

'You need to be discreet in your job, as I do in mine,' Tina agreed. 'But sometimes it can be helpful to discuss things with a friend, I agree.

'Obviously there will be a little package under the tree in their suite on Christmas morning. I'm sure it will be jewellery she can wear with her new dress.

'And Mrs Maitland has told me what she's bought for her husband to unwrap on the big day.'

'Is it something jokey, like the gifts the Royal Family apparently give one another at Christmas? A whoopee cushion, maybe?'

'Perish the thought! Summer's gift to Mr Maitland on their wedding day was a gold and pearl tie pin. I've seen him with it on and it's very classy.

'He loves wearing it and, though he doesn't know, Mrs Maitland has bought him a gold ring with a seed pearl inset. It will be as good a match as possible with his tie pin.

'How the other half lives, eh?'

All Ashore

After the show finished Noah changed and set off for Reception. He still hadn't invited Carys to go ashore with him in Porto Claro.

He found her mentor on duty.

'Hi, Noah? How was the show?' Mark looked up from a list.

'Captive audiences are always good.' Noah grinned. 'Beats me how they put up with me!'

Mark shook his head.

'Pull the other one. Some of our lady passengers have been known to catch two performances in the same evening!

'My mum's a fan and she's mad that she couldn't get a booking on this cruise. She left it late as Dad had been poorly.'

'I'm sorry. I hope he's better now. Be sure to remind me and I'll sign a photo for you to take back with my best wishes.'

'Thanks! Mum will be thrilled to bits.'

'Is it too late to book for the shore excursion tomorrow?' Noah clasped his hands behind his neck and stretched. 'I could do with some serious walking.'

'We still have places, especially on the earlier boats.' Mark adopted the smooth tones of a travel commentator. 'You'll alight on a sun-bleached jetty to the happy sound of a steel band beneath a blue sky while you receive a warm welcome from the locals.

'And the weather forecast is great for tomorrow. I know Carys is taking her first-ever trip ashore on the nine o'clock transport.' He gave the singer a sly look. 'Shall I put you down for the same time or is it too early?'

'It's not too early and yes, please add me to the list. To be honest I've been hoping to ask if she'd like to make the trip with me.'

Suddenly he felt awkward.

'I don't want to embarrass her.'

'I very much doubt that would happen, especially when every other female on this ship will be green with envy.'

'That's the lovely thing about Carys. When we first met she hadn't a clue who

I was. Boy, was I pleased!

'You can't imagine how it feels to get to know someone who has no preconceived ideas about you.'

'It can't be easy, meeting up, given the odd hours the pair of you work. Typical of cruise-ship life as I know.'

'No, it isn't easy but I can't wait to see her tomorrow. I gather Porto Claro is a particularly lovely island?'

'All the islands we sail around are beautiful. My own favourite is White Keys.

'My fiancée and I are booked for that excursion and I hope we can buy her an engagement ring in one of the boutiques.'

Noah whistled.

'Congratulations! Is your fiancée taking a cruise holiday or does she work on board?'

'She works in the beauty salon. I proposed to her in Marquisa and, luckily for me, she accepted.'

'Great news!' Noah turned his head. 'You have another customer so I'll beat it.'

'You report here tomorrow morning at quarter to nine. Crew members will be waiting to escort everyone to their launch.

'Be sure to book yourself on a return boat and take note what time the last one will depart the island.'

'Could you put me down to return on the one Carys has booked, providing it gets me back in time for the show? I don't think I'm quite ready to become a beach bum yet!'

Noah headed out to the deck. He'd walk his usual circuit then have a snack and a drink.

Now that tomorrow was sorted all he had to hope was that Carys would be pleased to see him.

Porto Claro

By half-past seven Carys was breakfasting. A dash back to her cabin for last-minute preparations and she was down at Reception on time.

Already a few passengers were waiting. Suzanne and another colleague were on duty but Carys kept out of the way.

She was wondering about Noah's comment about going ashore when a familiar voice spoke her name.

She turned to see the singer, dressed in T-shirt and shorts and carrying a small rucksack as she was.

'Hello.' She smiled at him, her heart bumpety-booming as if trying to escape her ribcage.

She knew the last thing she needed was to fall for a man who was idolised by countless other women. But it was lovely to see Noah and, after all, they were a team, in a way.

'I took the liberty of booking for the same departure as you.'

He was standing so close she could detect the tang of aftershave, possibly with an undertone of sun lotion. She felt almost tongue-tied.

One of her colleagues, probably Mark, must have told him what time she was going. It didn't matter.

She and Noah were temporarily adrift from the real world so why not enjoy his company while she could?

'I'm pleased you're here.'

She looked up at him and when he bent to kiss her cheek it seemed perfectly natural.

'You look very pretty this morning, my lovely.'

She clicked her tongue.

'Thank you. I hate to say it but you haven't got the Welsh accent quite right.'

'OK. I love the way you speak, by the way. I wasn't making fun of you.'

Carys wondered whether he'd heard from his London contact but this wasn't the time for serious discussion. Especially when she felt so happy in knowing he wanted to spend time ashore with her.

They waited their turn to board the launch as *The Golden Goddess* was too big to tie up at Porto Claro's harbour so it had anchored a little way out.

Carys suddenly became overwhelmed by the expanse of sea around her but there were helping hands available and, as she sat beside Noah, he reached for her hand and squeezed it comfortingly.

'I expect you find it strange that I should take a job at sea when I'm so clueless about boats?' she confessed.

'Not at all. I don't suppose many air stewards and stewardesses can fly an aeroplane, after all. Can you swim?'

She laughed.

'I can but you wouldn't enter me in the Olympics! I've brought my bikini, though.'

'Great!' He cleared his throat. 'I mean because I have my swimming kit with me, too.'

Before long they were tying up at the jetty.

'Your colleague, Mark, gave me the tour guide's version of arriving here,'

Noah said. 'He wasn't exaggerating!'

Carys gazed around.

'It looks gorgeous.'

Once ashore the two set off, hand in hand. Carys felt excited at visiting somewhere so exotic but wondered whether her escort might think her a little naïve.

Noah must have seen many countries, experienced many different cultures.

She said as much.

'I've visited lots of cities all over,' he replied, 'but I've not had much time to explore. Except for when I did a stint in New York.

'That was different because I shared a flat with two other guys and we did as much sightseeing and partying as we could.'

He smiled.

'This island is amazing. They must have suffered from the tidal wave that hit this area but you wouldn't know.'

'Last summer, wasn't it?'

'It was. Now, I could murder a cold drink. That beach bar over there looks tempting. Would you care to join me, señorita?'

'Why, thank you, señor. While we're sitting down how about you tell me if there's any news from your friend, Luke?'

'Excellent idea. And then let's forget everything and just enjoy being together.'

★ ★ ★

Noah ordered their drinks and sat back in his chair, thinking how fresh and pretty Carys looked in her pink summer dress.

This girl who'd entered his life so unexpectedly was unlike any other.

What he told Mark at Reception was true. Carys couldn't care less about his fame and he guessed she had had to ask around to learn about his career.

They smiled across the table at each other.

'Thanks for keeping me company.'

'That works both ways. So, any news?'

'My detective friend is examining the Rupert Maitland Holdings accounts. Also, he's got to know a lady who works in their accounts department.

'This employee is very concerned with how the company's being run and was friendly with the previous company secretary. Her husband worked with Simon Waters some years back.'

'Does she know he is still missing?'

'Obviously I told Luke what I witnessed.' Noah replied. 'I've no idea whether he's mentioned it to her or not. Probably not; he's very discreet and professional.'

'It hasn't caused as much gossip as I imagined it would,' Carys marvelled. 'Interesting, considering we have a well-known journalist on board.'

'You think that significant? What if Summer knew Mr Waters was on board and Rupert confessed his part in what happened that night?

'That would make the famous Summer Breeze an accessory after the fact.'

Noah pulled a face.

'I hope not. That would put her in a very precarious position. Falsifying accounts is a serious offence.

'Anyway, how about we finish our drinks and get going? You can decide where we should go first.'

A Kiss in the Rain

The pair set off hand in hand as they had before.

Heading away from the beach they wandered around the shops and stalls, peering at locally produced clothing and bright scarves in lemon, tangerine and emerald green.

They found a turquoise shade they both agreed matched exactly the sea sparkling in the distance and marvelled at elegant sculptures carved from tree roots, all beautifully crafted.

Some of the stallholders and shop-keepers were working while waiting for customers and, inside a jeweller's shop, Noah noticed that Carys had fallen in love with a turquoise and silver ring.

She tried it on the little finger of her right hand before taking a glance at the price ticket.

She sighed and handed the ring back to the shop owner.

'It's beautiful and it fits perfectly but

I'll have to leave it, I'm afraid. Maybe some other time.'

Noah knew better than to insist on buying it for her but he resolved to find a way to do so later, even if he was forced to concoct some ridiculous excuse.

If he could, he'd keep the ring until the end of the cruise. At least, then, he would have something to give her to mark the time they'd spent together.

The thought filled him with regret but it also made him all the more determined to make the most of their hours together today and any more stolen time they might manage to find in the future.

They discovered a beautiful gallery which was crammed with watercolours and paintings in oil. All reflected the exotic flowers and shrubs which splashed the island with bright colours, achingly white blossoms and lush green foliage.

'Do you think you could flag down a taxi?' Carys asked when they left the shops. 'There are some botanic gardens which I fancy seeing if that would be OK with you?'

'No problem,' he told her.

In fact it took a while before one came along and, when it did, they were surprised to find they would be sharing it with other passengers.

Jammed into the back seat Noah longed to place his arm around Carys's shoulders but he decided not to crowd her.

Palm Tree Haven was only a few kilometres away. The pair wandered around the gardens enjoying cones of mango ice-cream while admiring all kinds of flowers, few of which either could identify.

It was as they stopped to admire a huge cloud of hibiscus blooms that Noah felt the first drops of rain. It was still warm but they were both unprepared for wet weather.

As if reading his mind, Carys smiled.

'Note to tourists — rain isn't unusual here in hot Decembers. Shall we shelter over there?'

She pointed to a palm tree a few yards away.

'Race you!'

On arrival, Noah put his arm around her shoulders and hugged her to him. She snuggled against his chest and, catching the sweet scent of shampoo, he buried his face in her hair.

Carys moved her head back so she was looking up at him and, without thinking or wondering whether he should ask permission, his lips met hers in a long, sweet kiss.

She locked her hands behind his neck as he held her tight.

There was still no-one else within sight as the kiss ended.

'I've been wanting to do that all morning,' Noah whispered. 'Not to mention every day since I first met you.'

'I've been wondering when you'd kiss me properly ever since that first time on deck,' Carys told him.

She traced her forefinger around the outline of his mouth and Noah drew her close again.

This time their kiss was more meaningful. His hands stroked her hair as he kissed her as though he never wanted to stop.

The rain drummed on the umbrella of palm fronds above and, when their second kiss ended, he and Carys looked up and laughed.

'Maybe not the best tree in the world for sheltering beneath,' he offered, patting her damp hair.

'It'll stop soon so maybe we should head for the beach then. I can't miss the chance to swim in the Caribbean and make my friends back home jealous!'

She raised her face towards his again, a blissful expression upon her face.

What was a guy to do? Noah kissed her a third time.

Caribbean Swim

'That taxi driver must have had a train to catch!' Noah said.

'I closed my eyes in places.' Carys admitted. 'Shall we walk further along the beach to swim?'

She'd seen a group of passengers from the ship and guessed Noah might prefer to go somewhere he was less likely to be approached.

They strolled along the boulevard, past cafés where people lingered over cool drinks or delicious Caribbean food. Carys felt she'd always remember this island's sounds, smells and colours.

They found a part of the beach with hardly anyone else around and each changed behind a cluster of rocks.

Carys was wearing her pink bikini beneath her summer dress but took a while to bundle her hair into a bathing cap.

Hand in hand they ran towards the water, splashing and yelling like two kids, until they decided to swim to a raft.

'If this is December I can live with it very well.' Carys sighed once they settled.

'Me, too.' Noah propped himself up on one elbow and looked down at her. 'Do you know you have a perfect sprinkling of freckles on the bridge of your nose?'

'Oh, no!' Carys sat up again. 'They shouldn't be coming out in December!'

'I think they suit you.'

'Well, I shouldn't be cross, not when I'm floating in the Caribbean with you.'

'I think I'm the lucky one.' Noah sat up and kissed her lightly on the mouth. 'Sadly, I think we should make a move soon.'

'I wish we could stay longer.'

'So do I, but duty calls.' He got to his feet and reached out to pull her up beside him. 'This is a strange romance, Miss Carys Lloyd-Smith.'

'I'm not complaining,' she teased.

He took her hands in his and kissed them.

'I wish we could have met under different circumstances.'

'Noah, we come from two different worlds. Can't we just enjoy being together while we have the chance?'

Noah grasped her hand and they jumped into the sea then swam back to the beach.

Carys felt uncertain. Was Noah becoming serious about her?

If he was she couldn't imagine the resulting complications. Yet, now they'd found one another, how could she bear to let him go?

'That Little Madam!'

During the show's interval Suki knocked on Noah's door, barged in and demanded to know where he'd been all day.

'Not that it's any of your business,' Noah said calmly, 'but I went ashore with Carys from the purser's office.'

Suki fished for a tissue and cried.

'You've done this before, you know it!'

'Sorry? What have I done before?'

'My friend was in the cast of 'Angel In Black Leather'. She told me about Georgie, how you made up your mind you wanted her. Look how well that turned out!'

'Thanks for your take on my past romance. I'm surprised you haven't put something in the ship's daily newspaper!'

'If I did maybe some of your fans wouldn't be so admiring!'

She faced him, hands on hips.

'Here you are, acting like a lovesick teenager. Yet I bet that girl gets off with a different guy every time a new lot of passengers comes on board!'

'That's enough!' Noah kept his voice low but Suki was trying his patience.

He didn't inform her this was Carys's first cruise. She'd make another nasty comment.

'Noah, surely you haven't forgotten how close we were while we were training?'

He felt a surge of annoyance.

'We were friends, Suki, that's all. You were always far too possessive. I can't help being who I am.

'Georgie and I were together for a year and I realise any girlfriend of mine gets a rough deal in many ways.'

'I'd like to know what's so special about what's her name!'

How was he to put that into words?

'She didn't have a clue about my profession when we met.' He couldn't help smiling. 'I found that refreshing.'

'Doesn't she get out much?'

Noah ignored the catty remark.

'Sweetie, all of us in the cast know how famous you are yet you're treated just like everyone else, aren't you? What's so different about the way she is with you?'

'I'm not prepared to discuss my feelings.'

'Suit yourself!' Suki rose. 'Mark my words, Noah, that little madam will finish with you when we sail back into Southampton and I won't be around to pick up the pieces!'

Hoping for a Miracle

'Good morning, Mark. Did you and your fiancée enjoy Porto Claro?' Carys had arrived bang on time as the clock above the reception desk showed 07.00 hours.

Her colleague beamed.

'You bet. We decided we might as well look for an engagement ring rather than wait till we get to White Keys.

'It took us a while but in the end we went back to see if the first one she tried on was still available. Luckily it was.'

'Is she wearing it yet?'

'No, she wants to wait until Christmas Day. You women are weird sometimes!'

'I don't think it's weird. It'll make December 25 really special as the day you formally became engaged to be married.

'One day you can bore your grandchildren with the story!'

'You have a point. Thanks, Carys.'

'Don't mention it. I keep promising

myself I'll make an appointment with Penny to have my hair trimmed.'

'She's a brilliant stylist. She cut my hair when I was in her cabin the other night.'

He looked flustered.

'I mean to say — I didn't mean I actually stayed all night with her! Will you stop laughing at me like that?'

'I'm not laughing at you, Mark. I'm pleased there are still gentlemen like you around, despite what people say about life in the Seventies.'

'I hope you haven't experienced any problems in that direction, Carys, though I can't imagine Noah misbehaving.

'I know you spent the whole of yesterday together.'

She shook her head.

'We got on very well. I can't imagine him behaving badly, either.'

'Your cheeks are turning pink. Just how well did the pair of you get on, I wonder.'

'This is like when I was a teenager, having my big brother question me about my boyfriend! I loved the island and we had fun, even when we had to rush to shelter from a sudden rainstorm.

'We had a lovely swim later and I really enjoyed my day.'

'I'm glad. But what was that I heard about you two only just making it back to the harbour to catch your transport?'

'News travels fast round here! Noah decided to return to a shop we'd visited that morning so I looked after our rucksacks while he ran there and back.

'I was panicking because he'd have been late for his performance if we'd missed our launch.

'Apparently, he saw something earlier and didn't buy it, then thought it'd make a perfect late Christmas gift for his mum.'

She turned away to greet a new arrival.

'How nice to see you, Mrs Brown. I haven't noticed you around for a few days. I hope everything's going well?'

Carys didn't know how to speak to this passenger. Last time she'd spoken to Lucy the mysterious disappearance of her new-found friend had been very recent.

'I've had a couple of rough days. Just a slight cold and generally out of sorts but I'm feeling much better now. I thought I'd show up early for breakfast.'

'I'm pleased to hear it. To my mind this is the best part of the cruise. I love sunshine!'

Lucy nodded.

'I'm sure you're not surprised to know I've been thinking a lot about Martin. I don't suppose you've heard anything?'

Carys saw the look in Lucy's eyes and her heart went out to her. She'd obviously been attracted to Simon, to give him his real name, and it must have been devastating to learn of his fate.

'I wish I could give you good news but as yet we've heard nothing, though people have been known to disappear and turn up a while later . . .' She knew how feeble that must sound.

Lucy was nodding.

'I know it's extremely unlikely that Martin will have escaped drowning,' she said. 'I fully realise that but I still feel sad about what might have been.

'And I still find myself hoping for a miracle. Do you think I'm crazy?'

'Not at all, I understand why you feel as you do.

'Have you made any friends to help comfort you, keep your mind off things?'

'Oh, yes, there are two ladies travelling together who have taken me under their wing and I'm enjoying the creative-writing sessions very much.

'I've begun my first short story, set on a cruise liner. The author's very helpful indeed.'

'Well done,' Carys encouraged her.

'I'm determined to give my story a happy ending.' Lucy Brown stepped back from the counter. 'Life goes on but I shan't stop hoping.

'I hardly had time to get to know him but I truly don't believe Martin took his own life.'

Biding His Time

To Noah's relief the next time he saw Suki she treated him as she treated the other men in the company.

With bearded Matt, certainly, she was very flirtatious and he was obviously enjoying her attentions.

Noah knew Suki hated being without a boyfriend and if Matt enjoyed being the chosen one that suited Noah well.

He'd joined a cruise liner to make his life less complicated, not more so.

But now he had found himself falling in love with someone determined not to let anything interfere with her dream job.

In addition the violent scene on deck he'd witnessed earlier in the voyage still concerned and intrigued him. There were so many unanswered questions.

He couldn't help wondering whether the man he'd seen hanging around, that time Summer hijacked his circuit of the deck, might have been Simon Waters.

Perhaps he had been shadowing Summer, hoping to find her in a romantic tryst with a man, then to be able to taunt Rupert.

Could he have suspected her of flirting with Noah? She had flung her arms around him, after all.

Or had he been following Summer but given up after Noah arrived? Many secrets had disappeared with him, secrets Rupert Maitland wouldn't wish made public.

If Luke's detecting skills could prove fraudulent activities on Maitland's part then justice would be done.

A series of events had caused Simon to fall overboard but it was significant that Rupert hadn't reported the tragedy. Why?

Because he'd be questioned as to what had led to Simon's fall. And he'd remained silent too long for him to confess the truth now, including Simon's true identity.

He was probably relieved to learn of the suicide theory but he did not know what was happening in the background.

That Noah was determined to discover the truth.

Maitland could be biding his time, uncertain whether or not he'd been recognised that night.

Noah himself had no idea whether Rupert had heard him yelling as he rushed off to sound the alarm.

If he had, wouldn't he wonder why the anonymous spectator hadn't set off a chain of investigation leading to Rupert's interrogation?

Mickey Mouse

A call had come through from the chief purser to the entertainment section for Noah. Andy said a fax had arrived and awaited his attention.

The moment there was a break in rehearsals the singer hurried to Reception and asked to speak to Andy.

Moments later he was sitting in Andy's office, reading the message from his detective friend.

When typing his letter Luke had changed certain names even though the letter was being sent direct to the machine in the chief's office.

This was highly confidential stuff.

He scanned the typed sheet.

To: Noah Darcy c/o The Golden Goddess
From: Luke Rossiter, London

Good morning.
Further to your inquiries about Mickey

Mouse Holdings I can now confirm the following:

The present company secretary of Mickey Mouse Holdings has, after much investigation, confirmed that there are serious discrepancies throughout the whole of its accounting system.

At the time of writing the police have been contacted. At some point I anticipate a senior Fraud Squad officer will fly out to the Caribbean and Mickey Mouse will be required to attend an interview at the nearest police station.

Obviously I can't confirm any date yet. The liner's itinerary will be studied and the detective's flight arranged so that the officer can board the cruise ship at the earliest opportunity.

They will liaise with the captain and chief purser regarding the removal of Mr Mouse for questioning.

I wish you well with your continuing voyage.

Kind regards,
Luke

Noah read the letter aloud to Andy.

'What did you think when this came through?'

Andy shook his head.

'I had no idea you were in touch with a private detective. I'm intrigued as to why but I do understand it's none of my business.

'This is obviously a very serious matter and we both know how important it is for nobody besides the two of us to learn what's going on.'

Noah was concerned.

'Carys has been aware of my position all along. Shouldn't I tell her?'

Andy considered.

'I don't think it advisable. This is a huge step forward in this whole affair and I can only repeat that nobody at all, including Carys, should be informed.

'She's not on duty until after lunch today so there's no way she'll know about your fax message.'

Noah took the letter back and tucked it inside his wallet.

'All right. Our Mr Mouse can't get off

the liner until we reach the next port of call, of course. But the detective may not be able to get there in time!

'If, by some remote chance, Mr Mouse discovered that the police were on his tail — pardon the pun — he could leave the ship and make his escape. 'Someone like him is bound to have worldwide contacts.'

Andy nodded.

'Exactly. White Keys is one of the more prosperous Caribbean islands and has its own airport.'

He placed a hand on Noah's shoulder.

'We're dealing with a very wealthy and important individual here. Whatever he has or hasn't done he is a passenger on this liner and neither the captain nor I have the right to keep him under lock and key when there's no proof of any wrongdoing.'

'But Andy . . . !'

'Enough, Noah. We don't know whether he's guilty or not. Unless he causes trouble he'll be treated with respect and attention.'

Noah nodded reluctantly.

'I understand. But you're aware of the link between Simon Waters and our VIP passenger as much as I am. Do you think he'll be questioned about that?'

'I do. After all, the Marquisa Police Department is in possession of your statement and will have faxed it to Scotland Yard.

'As far as we're aware you were the only witness to the fight and to their conversation. Still, even you can't be one hundred per cent certain the fall overboard was caused by our suspect.'

Noah groaned.

'If only I felt confident enough to swear on the bible that he was the person I saw on deck that dreadful night.'

'Yes, or Simon Waters would turn up ready to tell his version of events! But that isn't going to happen.'

Proof Positive

Carys arrived for her shift resolved to make one final check of the arrangements for Summer's birthday celebrations.

She glanced up and saw Rupert emerging from the elevator. Could he be on his way to her desk?

Her mouth dried as he came towards her. This was the moment she could mention the tie pin without Summer hearing.

'Good afternoon, sir,' she greeted him cheerfully. 'I'm just checking everything's in order for Friday.'

Her heart was pumping faster than it should but she couldn't just blurt out what she wanted to say.

'Good afternoon, um, Carys. And is all well regarding my wife's big day?'

'Yes, everything should go smoothly. We have an excellent team who'll all do their best to give your wife a magical birthday.'

'That's good to hear.'

'Actually, Mr Maitland, there's something I've been meaning to ask you.'

He raised his eyebrows.

'Speak.'

She swallowed hard and asked the question that had intrigued her for so long.

'You think whatever's been found might belong to me?' he responded, puzzled. 'Well, my gold cufflinks and the like are, to the best of my knowledge, in a satin-lined box locked inside our stateroom's safe.'

Carys nodded.

'Would you mind putting my mind at rest, though? The item happens to be a tie pin. You do wear a tie pin on occasion?'

'I do, but I only brought one with me as it's rather special.'

'I apologise for troubling you but company regulations require us to ask anyone who might have lost something to describe the item in question.'

'I understand. Mine has an inlaid pearl — a Russian one, I believe — set

177

in a thick, gold bar. On the back of the bar is a tiny engraving which my wife decided upon as it was a gift from her.

'Unfortunately I broke the safety chain a while back and neglected to have a new one added. I wear the pin only when I'm in evening dress.'

She watched as his confident expression changed, almost crumbling as if some mechanism was whirring and clicking into place.

'That sounds satisfactory, Mr Maitland.'

'Well, let's take a look at what's been handed in. I can't see much point, though.'

Carys flew into the inner office and grabbed the key to the drawer. He'd given such a detailed description and she felt a moment of triumph that her hunch had been right.

Holding the pin in her hand and heading back to the desk she was relieved to find Rupert still waiting.

She placed the tie pin on the counter before him and he looked stricken as he snatched at the pin, cradling it in his hands.

'I'm not sure what's going on. I was convinced this was in the safe but this is definitely mine.

'Could someone have got into our suite, I wonder.'

His perplexed expression was a sham and Carys knew it.

She also knew Rupert was fully aware the liner's luxury accommodation was perfectly secure. The codes for accessing the personal safe in each suite were changed after passengers moved out and new numbers were put in place when the next guests moved in.

He looked flustered. Time to unsettle him further?

'Rest assured, sir, that couldn't have happened. The tie pin is obviously the one you described.

'Maybe, the last time you wore it, it somehow became loose and fell on to the deck. Do you recall being jostled or bumped into by anyone?'

The colour had drained from his face.

'Do you know when this was found, Carys?' he asked instead.

It was interesting how easily her name came to him when he was on the spot.

'It was handed in a few days ago.'

He blinked hard then took out a large white handkerchief and wiped his forehead before reaching for his wallet and placing his tie pin inside it.

'Are you all right, Mr Maitland? Shall I fetch you a glass of water?'

'No, I'm fine, thank you. Just stunned at my own stupidity. I must have lost my tie pin without realising it, then forgot I'd been wearing it once we got back to our suite.'

Carys knew he had seen his wife into the elevator before going on deck alone. There was no 'we' involved.

'You've been very kind, Carys, and thank you for all your efforts.' He tried for a calmer tone. 'I hope Summer doesn't suspect what we've cooked up for her.'

He turned away from the desk just as Noah arrived.

Falling Out

'Good morning!' Noah said.

The tycoon gave a brief nod to the singer but didn't reply.

'Rude devil! That's him, isn't it?' Noah watched Rupert waiting to enter the elevator.

'Yes. He's just collected his missing tie pin which he claims he thought was still locked away in his suite.

'More importantly, does this mean you identified him from having seen him that one time, Noah?'

'Definitely. Of course, I've glimpsed him sitting beside Summer in the theatre a couple of times but I've never been able to study his face.

'Thinking back to that moment when he glanced up at me from the deck below, and having seen him in broad daylight just now, I'm sure it's the same man.'

He shrugged.

'It would be difficult for a jury to convict him on the strength of my evidence, though. Remember, too, he didn't actually push Simon Waters overboard.'

'But we know Simon had a very good reason for confronting him.'

Noah nodded.

'Simon was the one who started the rough stuff, though.'

'I get that, but I can understand why he was furious enough to attack Rupert,' she replied.

'I can, too. But the fact remains that, after Simon launched himself to attack, Rupert staggered back because the ship listed. Simon toppled over the rail without any help from Rupert.

'The verdict would probably be death by misadventure, wouldn't it?'

Carys sighed.

'I suppose so but it makes me so angry to think of Rupert denying Simon's accusations and getting away with his nefarious activities.'

Noah glanced around to make sure nobody was within earshot.

'There's no chance he'll get away with the kind of financial jiggery-pokery he's been up to. Believe me!'

'Jiggery-pokery?'

'Fraud. Sharp practice.' He grinned. 'Not a Welsh expression, then, look you?'

'If it is I've never heard it. And that's a terrible accent! Is that what I sound like? I hope not.'

She had such a gorgeous chuckle.

Noah had had to take a deep breath when she leaned over the counter to whisper back to him. Being close to her, catching that lemony drift from her hair was an absolute joy.

But she was still curious.

'Noah, you know something, don't you? Have you been in touch with Luke?'

He hesitated, remembering Andy's warning.

'Your boss handed me a message from him but there's nothing concrete to tell you yet.'

'It must have included something your detective friend thought important enough for you to know, surely?'

'It did, but I'm sworn to secrecy, Carys. I'm sorry.'

He hated excluding her but daren't ignore Andy's advice.

'I see.' She moved away from the counter. 'Sorry I asked.'

He spread his hands in frustration.

'Look, this isn't our game, you know that. I was anxious to find out about Maitland because I felt uncomfortable.

'It might have been that he had an accomplice on board who could have tipped *me* over the rail some dark night if Rupert feared my recognising him.

'Plus I felt sorry for Simon. I don't like to see little guys pushed around by big ones.'

'That's very commendable but it's clear I can't be trusted to know what's going on.

'And now Rupert has his wretched tie pin back and he'll have put it into the safe, so no-one will ever learn what we know. It's not fair!'

'Carys!'

But she had turned away, heading for the other side of the desk.

'Sorry to keep you waiting, madam.

How may I help?'

Noah shook his head and walked away. She was understandably miffed because he wasn't acknowledging her as part of a team but he still felt he had done the wise thing by involving his pal.

Luke's contact within Rupert's company had proved invaluable in providing some background knowledge. The lady in the office would, no doubt, be devastated when she heard about her friend Simon's fate.

Noah felt keener than ever to see Rupert Maitland taken away for questioning when the British police officer boarded the cruise ship.

As for Carys, well, hopefully she'd come round. He himself faced a hectic few days because of the Christmas festivities, not to mention rehearsals for extra shows catering for eager audiences who couldn't get enough of musical theatre.

He and the gang would be performing scenes from the old classic, 'Holiday Inn'.

Noah knew that would go down a

storm with the vast majority of the passengers who were known privately, if affectionately, as the Silver Cruisers.

To make matters worse Suki would be his co-star. Talk about bad timing!

He had absolutely no wish to become closer to the attractive dancer but if Carys wanted to see the show — and he knew how much she loved old movies — she could be made unhappy by seeing him take Suki in his arms.

This might be a good thing, he reflected. If their relationship was to develop Carys would have to learn to accept Noah's leading ladies and trust him to remain true to her.

He wanted that very much even though he knew it was far too early in their relationship to declare his feelings.

At this moment he felt sad, knowing their relationship had taken a backward step today.

Festive Fun

Conscious of the excitement building as the big day neared Carys tried to push away all her doubts and misgivings.

Christmas decorations gleamed and sparkled all around the main passenger areas and a special pine tree awash with tinsel, glittering ornaments, coloured lights and pink and white candy canes was a huge favourite with children accompanying their parents and grand-parents on this very special cruise.

For Carys, Christmas would be a sad one if she and Noah were still at a distance.

Once the liner reached White Keys on December 23 there would be a three-night stopover. An afternoon carol concert in the music theatre was planned for Christmas Eve. It would be led by Noah and the other vocalists along with a group of passengers who had been practising together.

Those wishing to go ashore could do

so but it was anticipated the vast majority would remain on board, enjoying the sumptuous menus, dancing and festive surprises.

On Christmas Day the children's entertainers would host a special afternoon so parents could linger in the restaurants longer than usual, knowing their youngsters were having fun with the experienced staff employed solely for the children's wellbeing.

Noah and the other performers would appear in three separate shows, each one hour long, between seven o'clock and midnight.

Meanwhile one of the stewards, dressed as Santa Claus, held court in one of the big lounges handing out small gifts to the children.

Despite all the Yuletide cheer and the general good mood Carys still felt as festive as a Christmas stocking left out in the rain.

She knew she shouldn't have shown her feelings to Noah as she had but she still found it hurtful to think he didn't trust her.

Maybe this was all for the best. They had been getting on a little too well for a couple whose days together were counting down as *The Golden Goddess* sailed towards another tropical island stopover.

Carys was ending a telephone call when she spotted Lucy Brown hovering beside the elevator. She gave her a friendly wave and at once the lady hurried forward.

'How are you, Lucy? I hope all this Christmas frenzy isn't too much for you?'

Lucy smiled.

'You're a very thoughtful young woman. I'm looking forward to the lovely entertainment and the delicious food, of course.

'I've palled up with an elderly gentleman who couldn't face being home alone for his first Christmas as a widower. We both enjoy crosswords and reading and we're planning to spend time with the two ladies I'm friendly with.

'I was wondering if I could share something with you, if you're not too busy.'

'Of course. Let's get away from the front of the desk.'

Carys moved round to the very end of the counter, picked up an information sheet about White Keys and pretended to be discussing it with Lucy.

'You may laugh at me but one of my new friends reads palms and last night she gave me a reading.'

'Goodness, I'm not sure I'd want to know my future!' Carys commented.

'No, no, it's not like Madame Zara predicting a tall, handsome stranger entering your life and predicting you'll cross the water to a country you've never even dreamed of visiting!

'I'm amazed by the accuracy of what she told me.'

Carys didn't want to dampen Lucy's enthusiasm but nor did she want her to be buoyed up by unrealistic hopes.

'I imagine this has something to do with Simon — sorry, I mean Martin.'

She hoped Lucy would think mistaking his name was merely a slip of the tongue. Carys had no idea how much

Simon Waters might have told his new friend about his former career problems.

She also doubted he'd have admitted to using an assumed name.

But Lucy's expression remained serene.

'My friend said there was a dark-haired man who'd been separated from me but who would soon re-enter my life.

'I've never confided in anyone but you that I know which passenger it was who disappeared without trace, nor that he and I were becoming close.

'So I feel really positive! I've always believed Martin was still alive even if the odds against that are high.'

'Well, who am I to say, Lucy? There's nothing wrong with being hopeful.'

Carys kept her voice low.

'I don't want you to get hurt, that's all.'

The older woman nodded but Carys decided she was looking better than she had done when first arriving at the desk with her query.

As long as her hopes weren't raised

unrealistically surely there could be no harm in looking on the bright side.

Lucy was checking the time.

'Thank you for listening, my dear. I'll go find a quiet corner and do some writing now.'

Carys was relieved at the change of subject.

'I forgot to ask how your short story was coming along.'

Lucy beamed.

'It's almost finished but it is going to need a lot of editing. We can read our work aloud in the final session except I'm not sure I'll be brave enough.

'It would be fantastic to have something published in one of my favourite magazines, though, so I'm determined to keep writing.'

'Well done. If I don't see you before Christmas Day I hope you enjoy all the celebrations.'

A Close-Knit Family

As he'd predicted rehearsals for the Christmas Day performances were keeping Noah busy.

Musical theatre was his great love and he enjoyed singing to his leading lady as though she was, in real life, the woman he loved most of all in the world.

It wasn't until the cast broke for tea that he wondered about how to smash the icy barrier separating him and Carys.

He knew he had upset her and doubted she'd even let him try.

Should he write a letter? What if she ripped it up without opening it?

Perhaps he should he confide in Andy. Noah agreed with him that keeping the latest developments from Carys was for her own safety.

If he and Carys weren't cruising the Caribbean but were living on dry land he'd be round to her place with a huge bouquet of flowers. Somehow he'd manage to make her see things from his point of view.

Sadly there seemed no chance of that happening.

Steve and one or two of the others were heading in his direction, carrying mugs of tea. Someone was offering round chocolate biscuits. He mustn't sit looking gloomy.

Nor should he eat biscuits, tempting though they were. Keeping his weight down was vital to his career and the reason for his walks on deck and visits to the gym.

'Penny for 'em!' Steve sat down. 'You know, that was a good impersonation of Bing. You should enter a talent contest!'

'Well, I'm glad Noah didn't enter the one that I won! I might never have got to where I have now if he had!' Tim, the youngest of the team, grinned at Noah.

Everyone was in a good mood despite hard work and long hours. Right from the beginning of the cruise they had begun to form a close-knit family.

Noah felt as though he stood on the brink of a precipice. He was sorely tempted to share Luke's progress update with Carys but his integrity was on the line.

He couldn't see any other way but to remain resolute.

If she ignored him between now and December 25 he would hand her the ring he had purchased after that and would leave the rest to Fate.

A Doctor Calls

Carys was convinced time was speeding up in this pre-Christmas period. One morning she awoke and realised this was the day of Summer Maitland's birthday celebration.

For a change it wasn't Noah who'd jumped into her waking thoughts and she lay there, wondering what this told her.

Maybe it meant she was paranoid about her job and was panicking she might somehow have messed up Rupert's schedule.

Later, at the desk, she noticed one of the florist's staff carrying a huge bouquet towards the elevator.

She turned as she heard a low whistle.

'Look at those flowers!' Mark stood behind her.

'No prizes for guessing who they're for,' Carys replied. 'Lucky lady.'

'Is she?'

'I should say most people would think so.'

'Would you want to be married to him, then?'

'Come on, Mark, he's probably older than my dad! No amount of money would tempt me into marriage with someone like Rupert Maitland.

'I'm probably the only member of the team who believes Summer really loves him. She must do, surely.'

'Who knows? Still, she's a big girl and she knew his track record when they got hitched.

'Good luck to them, anyway. Without people like the Maitlands we probably wouldn't have a job. Their kind are always going to want to travel in style, to hand over wads of cash for the opportunity to be pampered.'

Carys thought of what might happen, not only to Rupert but also to Summer who, despite what Mark believed, might be unaware of her husband's financial track record.

If Rupert was forced to explain the devious practices of which he'd been accused her life could change dramatically.

It would also be an enormous test of her love for her husband.

'Hey, why the troubled look? Did you forget to have breakfast?'

'Sorry, Mark. Someone walking over my grave, I suppose.'

'How are things going with you and our star performer? Or shouldn't I ask?'

'Best not to, I'm afraid. Anyway, while it's quiet is there anything special you want me to do?'

'Now you mention it . . .'

He went into the inner office and returned with one of the long lists without which they all reckoned the ship wouldn't function.

Carys sat at the counter and set about her task while Mark made some phone calls.

She had soon learned the importance of team work and had decided it was a two-edged sword. You had the comfort of knowing someone had your back but, if you were the weakest link, you could let everyone else down.

No way would she have missed this

experience, though. Even though she hadn't bargained on falling in love with an impossible man at the same time well as falling in love with her new career!

Mark was still using the office line when Carys took a call on the desk phone.

'Hello, may I speak to the chief purser, please?'

She heard a lovely lilt in the woman's voice.

'I'm afraid he's not in his office just now. Can I get him to call you back?'

'How long will he be?'

'He should be back by nine o'clock. Who's calling, please?'

'I'm ringing from St Saviour's Hospital on the island of White Keys. Ask him to call Doctor Florence Portillo on this number, please.'

Carys wrote down the information and closed the call, wondering what all that was about.

A sudden thought struck her, one she didn't want to contemplate as being true. What if there was some dreadful outbreak of illness on the island?

What if the hospital was contacting all cruise liners heading in that direction?

She took a couple of deep breaths to regain her composure. All she could do now was leave the message on Andy's desk to read on his return.

She didn't have much longer to wait. Andy returned soon after nine o'clock and called to her immediately after picking up his message.

'Carys, did you take this phone call?'

'Yes, Andy. The switchboard probably tried your number but the call came through to the desk.'

'It's all right, you haven't done anything wrong. I just wondered what it was about, is all.'

She shook her head slowly.

'I've no idea. Could it be something to do with documentation?'

'Doubtful — we're well known on White Keys and I think it would be a port official calling us rather than a doctor.

'Well, I'd better find out what they want.' He hesitated. 'Forgive me for asking, but are you feeling all right?'

'I'm fine, thanks. What makes you ask?'

He considered.

'It's just that you haven't seemed quite your usual self recently. Apologies if I'm out of order, Carys.

'There is no problem with your work. We're more than happy with your performance.'

She swallowed a lump in her throat.

'Thank you, that's good to hear. Let's just say I'm a little bit in limbo at the moment but I shan't let it distract me.'

He nodded.

'As I say I'm not questioning your efficiency. If this is a matter of the heart I hope it's sorted out soon — for both your sakes.'

He disappeared into his office, closing the door behind him.

Astounding News!

As he set off to see Andy, Noah wondered what he'd done to cause the chief purser to ask him to call by.

He couldn't think of anything and hoped there hadn't been a complaint about his performance. With the current chilly relationship between Carys and himself, and Christmas looming, Noah could do without extra problems.

As soon as he arrived Mark greeted him and opened up the counter flap to let him go through. He tapped on the chief's door and went inside only to see Carys already sitting opposite Andy.

'Noah, take a seat. Thank you for coming at such a busy time.

'I asked Carys to be present as you both deserve to know what I've discovered today from a doctor involved in this rather astonishing situation.'

Noah looked sideways at Carys. She gave him the glimmer of a smile — a small gesture but enough to make him feel there might be a chink in the barrier between them.

Right now he needed to concentrate on what Andy was saying.

'Brace yourselves.' Andy looked from one to the other.

'Our friend Simon Waters, aka Martin Cooper, was found alive in the water not long after falling from this liner! Yes, you may well look astounded!

'Before I continue we need to remember that the main reasons people fall off cruise ships are taking their own life, drunkenness or foul play.

'We have to assume our survivor went overboard because of the last reason.

'The fact that he was picked up quickly was definitely a lucky outcome. He managed to stay afloat and, not long after he fell, he was picked up by a fishing boat heading for a night stop at an island too small for any cruise liner to visit.'

Carys gasped.

'Unbelievable!'

'My thoughts exactly,' Andy told her. 'Anyway the casualty, having been rescued, soon lost consciousness and was taken to a medical facility when the fishing boat reached harbour.

'Someone must have been knowledgeable enough to make sure Mr Waters was well wrapped up. By the sound of it he was savvy enough not to panic once he hit the water, thereby vastly increasing his chances of staying alive long enough to be rescued.

'It may well be that the air-sea rescue service we alerted would have found him had the fishing boat not turned up first.

'Mr Waters remained in a critical condition which led to him being taken to White Keys where he could be treated at a hospital with better facilities.'

Carys leaned forward.

'I'm sorry to interrupt, Chief, but didn't anyone connect him with the passenger reported missing from *The Golden Goddess*?'

'Good question, Carys. The fishermen wouldn't have had a clue and sometimes, in these parts, formalities can take a while.

'It also appears no documents of any kind, certainly nothing to link him with this ship, were found upon his person.'

'I'm still reeling at the thought of him having survived such a dreadful ordeal!' Noah commented.

Andy nodded.

'He was lucky not to have fallen into a freezing cold sea, certainly, but I think he must also have been in excellent health to have come through this.

'Apparently once he regained consciousness he was able to tell his story, though there are some gaps in his memory.

'Doctor Portillo, with whom I spoke, gives him a good prognosis.'

Carys could wait no longer.

'Please, are we allowed to tell his friend Lucy that he's alive? That lady has had faith all along that, somehow, he had survived.'

'No, we must follow protocol. The British Commission covering the eastern Caribbean will carry out the necessary research and they'll then contact the next of kin.'

The chief looked at Noah.

'I think it's time to inform Carys about your friend Luke's findings, Noah.'

'Definitely.'

Swiftly Andy outlined the plan for the police to meet the liner on Christmas Eve after they docked at White Keys.

'This, of course, means I must emphasise that this matter requires complete secrecy.

'With regard to Lucy Brown I know you're disappointed, Carys. You understand I have to act on behalf of the cruise line and will need to contact my superiors for guidance.'

'Of course. I'll say nothing to Lucy until you give permission. I know she'll be very happy to hear the news. What a miracle!'

'I hope the poor fellow's fit enough to sail back to Southampton with us,' Noah said.

Carys gasped.

'That hadn't occurred to me. If I'd

escaped drowning like that I'm not sure I could bear to get on a ship ever again!'

Waterworks

Carys was about to go off duty when Tina called at the desk to report she'd delivered Summer's heavenly cocktail dress.

'Mrs Maitland's having a wonderful day,' the stewardess said. 'I helped her get ready and she insisted I had a small glass of champagne to celebrate her birthday.

'Don't say I told you that!'

'My lips are sealed.' Carys thought how true that statement was.

The day after next the liner would dock at White Keys where it would remain while the passengers enjoyed traditional Christmas festivities onboard.

She felt sorry for Summer, having such a fantastic 40th-birthday celebration only then to receive an awful shock as she saw her husband led away by the British Fraud Squad officer.

Carys realised Tina was speaking.

'Hello, ground to Carys! What were

208

you thinking, I wonder.'

'Oh, um, just about birthdays in general. Sorry, what were you saying?'

'That Mr Maitland doesn't seem quite his usual self. He's much more withdrawn than he was. I hope he isn't coming down with something just on the verge of Christmas.'

'So do I! Maybe he's had a little too much bubbly?'

'Ah, I hadn't thought of that. He was certainly taking a rest while I was with his wife.'

Seeing Carys's attention was elsewhere Tina turned around and spotted who was approaching.

'Looks like Noah's heading for you so I'll catch you later, maybe? Are you eating with the passengers or in the mess?'

'Oh, the mess, I hope. About seven?'

Her friend went on her way. Suzanne was taking over from Carys and it seemed Noah wasn't budging until Carys noticed him.

'Five minutes,' she mouthed and went off to speak to her colleagues before going off duty.

As soon as she left the desk Noah walked towards her.

'Could we talk?'

He'd had his hair cut. She'd noticed it earlier when they were in with Andy. It was well trimmed but she preferred it longer.

She dragged herself back to the present and saw he looked as nervous as she felt.

'I'm happy to talk,' she said.

'Good. Do you want to go to the bar or shall we take a walk?'

He smiled and Carys thought he looked more relaxed already.

'I could do with a drink — something long and cool.'

'Let's go this way, then.'

Neither said a word until they reached the crew bar.

'How about over there?' Noah pointed to a table in the corner. 'And what can I get you to drink?'

'Could I have a white wine spritzer, please?'

'Of course.'

Carys looked around her as he left. All of a sudden it hit home that Christmas was so close she could almost taste it.

With weather almost as hot as Britain's summer had been this year it seemed surreal to see festive garlands twined around the bar and everywhere else possible.

The tree by the entrance stood in a red and green tub, its branches festooned with gold and silver baubles and shimmering tinsel. A large star gleamed at the top.

The loudspeaker system was crooning 'Have Yourself A Merry Little Christmas'.

Carys felt a surge of emotion. What was the matter with her? As she searched for a handkerchief Noah arrived.

'They're bringing my pot of tea over,' he announced, placing her glass before her.

'Hey, what's up?'

He reached in his pocket, brought out a snow-white handkerchief and handed it to her before sitting down and putting his arm around her shoulders.

'What is it, darling?'

Only four little words but what an effect they had! She leaned into him and sobbed.

'I never realised I had such a devastating effect on women,' Noah joked while cuddling her to him so tenderly she sobbed again.

'And I never realised I could laugh and cry at the same time.' Carys mopped up her tears. 'Gosh, I didn't mean to wreck your handkerchief.'

'No problem and I don't need it back. My mother gave me dozens of the things to pack. But I don't like seeing you so upset.'

'Blame the music. Listening to it must have set me off.'

Noah nodded.

'Music can have a powerful effect on the emotions and that song's one of my favourites. I'm not surprised you're feeling a bit weepy being away from home at this time of year.'

He hesitated.

'Hearing what your boss had to say was great but it also makes me fearful about our friend, Mickey Mouse, and what he might still have up his sleeve.'

He looked up as a young man delivered his tea.

'Thank you so much, Aijaz.'

The barman beamed and sped off again. Noah opened a packet of cheese and onion crisps and offered them to her.

'I prefer these to caviar!' he confessed.

She laughed.

'Thanks but I'll be eating soon. I don't want to think about the danger you might have been in, Noah, but I've also been wondering how the situation might affect Summer. How it's going to upset her Christmas.'

She picked up her spritzer.

'Gosh, that's better. Sorry again for the waterworks.'

'No need to apologise.'

'Oh, I think there is.' She put down her glass and reached for his hand. 'I behaved like a spoiled brat, having a tantrum because you wouldn't tell me what you'd heard from London.

'You were absolutely right to say nothing. I wasn't thinking straight before.'

He made no attempt to retrieve his hand, in fact she felt him squeeze hers back. It gave her a warm feeling as well as making her relieved they could discuss things comfortably once again.

'I know you would never have gossiped, Carys, but I think I wanted to shield you anyway. In consulting my friend I was taking a chance and it's a relief to know we've come this far.

'If Nick had discovered Mr Mouse had a record of violence I would have been paranoid about him creeping up on me one night and throwing me overboard.'

Carys shuddered and he hugged her.

'He's a very powerful man in every sense of the word. If he'd caught me unawares I wouldn't have stood a chance. No pun intended but I really do hope it's plain sailing from now onwards.'

She groaned.

'I'll forgive you though thousands wouldn't! So, friends again?'

They were holding hands. Some of Noah's fellow performers were sitting a few yards away and obviously longing to know what was going on.

'Are we friends again? I'd say yes, you bet we are.

'Unless you make my day, Carys, and tell me you'd prefer to be something more than that. I'd like that very much indeed.'

In Love

Back in her cabin Carys didn't know which made her feel more jittery — the liner's steady progress towards White Keys, where Rupert Maitland hopefully would receive his comeuppance, or deciding what to tell Noah next time they met.

After he'd hinted about taking their friendly relationship further she'd asked for a little more time to think about it.

'Take as long as you want,' he'd said. 'I'm planning on staying with this cruise until we dock at Southampton, touch wood.'

He'd knocked his knuckles on the wooden table top, reminding her that showbiz folk were often very superstitious.

He had made no effort to hold her hand once they got up from the table and had escorted her to the door before joining his friends. She wondered if they'd tease him.

What was stopping her from committing herself to being his steady girlfriend? Her sensible, practical side was battling her romantic, dreamy side and truthfully she didn't know which would win.

She still couldn't believe how such an attractive, talented man could fall for an ordinary girl like her.

Once she'd changed out of uniform, she headed for the mess, wondering if she was hungry enough to eat.

To her disappointment there was no sign of Tina but as Carys approached the food counter to make her choice she heard her friend's voice.

'Tina, I'm so glad to see you! I could do with some advice.'

'Might this concern a certain Mr Darcy?'

'Maybe.' Carys grinned. 'I wouldn't dream of talking about him to anyone else but you.

'Andy was right when he told me he thought you and I would hit it off.'

'He knows me so well. I usually take a while to feel comfortable with people but when I saw you in the queue to check in you looked like my kind of person.'

'It's difficult to make close friendships outside of work when we have such long hours.' Carys shook her head.

'Yes, it is. Hey, we'd better choose our food. There's a bunch of people coming in.'

Tina chose Caribbean fish curry while Carys opted for fried chicken with vegetables. They found a table and settled themselves.

Carys realised how hungry she was now she had the chance to relax. While they ate she confided in her friend and spoke of how she and Noah had settled their differences.

'I'm pleased for you,' Tina said. 'So what's the problem? Is he, er, too forward?'

Seeing Carys's expression she shrugged.

'Hundreds of females on board this ship would be glad to face that dilemma!'

Carys laughed even though she felt herself blush.

'Noah behaves like a perfect gentleman, although, thankfully, not too perfect in certain respects.'

Somehow she found it difficult to pour out her heart but they managed to finish their meals and decided to move on to the crew bar. Carys ordered her second white wine spritzer of the day plus one for Tina.

She had no intention of drinking too much, not when there were important matters to sort out.

They settled at a table near the door and her friend wasted no time.

'Right, why don't you tell Auntie Tina all about it?'

Carys described how thrilled she had felt when Noah talked about their relationship. 'He's giving me the chance to say how I feel and I appreciate that. But isn't he being unrealistic? It's not like he's a permanent entertainer on *The Golden Goddess*. He'll leave the ship at Southampton and I'll be working the next cruise.

'Our careers are similar in that it's

hard to have a normal social life. That never struck me as important when I applied for my job.

'I never dreamed I'd fall in love with a musical theatre star.'

She stared at Tina, open-mouthed.

'What did I just say?'

'You know very well! You don't need me to tell you how you feel about Noah.

'You can't shut love off like a tap, Carys. You'll only make yourself miserable — and him, too, by the sound of it.'

Carys shook her head vehemently.

'What chance would we have, Tina? Noah will go into the West End again or tour in something that'll take him all over the British Isles, or even abroad. He could end up on Broadway!

'No. For the sake of his career I'm going to have to tell him our relationship can only be a friendly one. Romance is not on the cards.'

Anguish

On the morning of Christmas Eve, Carys went to work realising what the expression 'a heavy heart' meant. She needed to speak with Noah but dreaded doing so.

Carys had spent much of the night reliving those hours spent with Noah on the beautiful island of Porto Claro.

Kissing him had felt so right. It had unlocked a part of her kept hidden until that magical day.

Never before had she felt this way about a man. When she'd blurted out that she'd fallen in love with the singer it had been because deep down she knew Noah was the one for her.

As she greeted people whose faces were now familiar and queued for eggs and coffee she told herself it was kinder to tell Noah their relationship must go no further.

She carried her tray to a table, trying to tell herself she'd made the right decision.

Noah had lived with his last girl-friend for a year before they split up. He and Carys couldn't do that even if she wanted to. Which she didn't. She was too traditional and mindful of her parents' feelings.

When she'd expressed her concerns Tina had told her she was thinking too hard.

Why couldn't Carys accept she'd fallen in love with a man who wanted to take things a step further than handholding and walks around the promenade deck?

'It's not like he's proposed!'

No, but Noah wanted a commitment. It was something she longed for, too, yet here she was, preparing to spoil his Christmas.

The thought of never being held in his arms again sent daggers through her heart but it must be done.

Only not today. There would be too much other stuff happening.

Andy would get that phone call from the local police station, would meet the Fraud Squad officer and escort him to the Maitlands' luxury suite.

Once Rupert was safely in custody Lucy would receive amazing news about the man she knew as Martin Cooper.

Many passengers would go ashore, buying last-minute gifts while soaking up the friendly island atmosphere. This Christmas Eve would be a significant one for several people and for varying reasons.

Carys didn't want to break Noah's heart. It was bad enough having to suffer her own anguish.

Under Arrest

The chief purser was behind the desk, talking to Mark, when Carys arrived for her seven o'clock shift. Andy greeted her.

'Thanks for being so punctual. I can brief you both at once now.'

No prizes for guessing what was happening. Carys knew this had been inevitable.

Having listened to Noah's account of the horrific accident she understood how ruthless the tycoon could be, even if he seemed soft as butter around his wife.

Rupert had made no attempt to call for help when his former employee fell overboard and he shouldn't be allowed to escape justice.

It sounded as if he'd done his utmost to intimidate Simon, both back in London and that night on deck.

Fortunately, once Rupert was in custody Noah wouldn't need to look over his shoulder for fear someone was sneaking up on him.

Andy was speaking, his face solemn.

'The fraud squad officer sent to arrest Rupert Maitland is in my office, drinking a cup of coffee.

'He suggested, in view of the circumstances, that he wouldn't be knocking on the Maitlands' door too early this morning. It isn't easy to predict how people will react when they find themselves being read their rights.

'He might go quietly, as they say, or he could make a fuss which might disturb other passengers. I told the officer I appreciated his consideration.'

'Mrs Maitland might be the one who reacts badly.' Mark was voicing Carys's own feelings. 'She won't forget this Christmas, poor woman.'

'Yes, well, this is how matters have worked out. Sentiment doesn't come into it where the police are concerned.'

'I hate to say this,' Mark commented, 'but I don't suppose our VIP passenger has done a bunk in the night? We did, after all, come into harbour in the small hours.'

Andy nodded.

'I took the precaution of asking the staff captain to order a crew member to position himself near the penthouse suites in case our suspect should decide to leave us, well, unexpectedly.

'No-one has emerged from any of those suites yet and I doubt Rupert Maitland had a boat waiting for him to jump from his balcony!

'Right, I'll collect our visitor and escort him to Penthouse Number One. Mark, could you pick up the duplicate key to gain access? Then I'd like you to accompany the officer and me, please.'

'Will do.'

Andy turned to Carys.

'This shouldn't take long. Are you happy to hold the fort?'

'Of course. I hope it all goes smoothly.'

'Thank you. I'm a mere onlooker but it doesn't feel good to know what one of our best customers is capable of.'

Carys watched the elevator swallow up the three men. She couldn't settle to anything and merely double-checked that the lists of passengers booked to go ashore were all in order.

She remained at the desk in case anyone needed attention.

Soon she saw the elevator doors slide open and Rupert Maitland, dressed casually and looking as disdainful as usual, stepped into the foyer, escorted by the Detective Inspector.

Rupert must be handcuffed, Carys thought, determined not to stare, but there was unlikely to be much interest at that time of day.

Andy obviously wanted to represent the cruise line in seeing Rupert disembark but Mark strode across the foyer to Carys, his face serious.

'How did it go?' she asked.

'The guy was amazingly calm. There was even a faint smile on his face when the DI read him his rights.

'You know, like you expect to hear in a TV crime series? It was weird knowing this was the real thing!'

'What about Summer? How did she react?'

'I think she was still in bed when Rupert came to the door. He had to be allowed into his bedroom to get dressed so his wife obviously knew what had happened.

'We locked the door behind us and Andy said he would ask Tina to check on Mrs Maitland — to make sure she didn't need treatment for shock or whatever.

'The whole thing was handled very efficiently in my opinion.'

Carys shivered.

'I hate to think of someone so wealthy and powerful riding roughshod over innocent people. Thank goodness Simon Waters was pulled out of the sea and is now recovering.'

Mark's eyebrows shot up.

'You seem to know a lot about all this, Carys.'

She shrugged.

'I only know because Noah confided in me after he saw two men struggling that night when he was standing on the balcony above.

'He had to give a statement to the Marquisa Police and he told Andy exactly what he'd seen.'

'So it was a kid-gloves situation?'

'Sort of,' Carys said. 'There was no actual proof that Rupert pushed anyone overboard.

'When Lucy Brown reported her concerns about a passenger she knew as Martin Cooper and who had seemed to vanish it seemed obvious that he was the missing man.'

Carys didn't intend to mention Noah's private detective friend's part in the operation. Nevertheless she felt Mark deserved an explanation as to how she knew so much about the incident.

It occurred to her that both Summer Maitland and Lucy Brown were going to remember Christmas 1976 for very different reasons.

Tears of Joy

Once Andy returned Carys asked when he planned to give Lucy Brown the good news.

'I have the authority to do that now so why don't you ring White Keys Hospital and say you're speaking on my behalf?' he suggested. 'See if they'll give you an update on — better get his name right — on the condition of Mr Simon Waters.

'If you have any problems put whoever it is through to me.'

Soon Carys was tapping on her boss's door.

'Mr Waters has responded well to treatment and is out of danger. But the ward sister wishes to speak to you.'

A few minutes later, Andy called her into his office and asked her to sit down.

'The good news is that our miracle man is allowed visitors for a short period today, though no more than two at a time.

'What they are concerned about is his state of mind and whether he should rejoin the ship and sail home with us, or if it would be more advisable for the company to pay for his flight back to London.'

Carys considered.

'What would you want to do if you were in his position?'

Andy sat down, clasped his hands behind his head and gazed at the ceiling.

'That's a tough question! I'm pretty sure I would opt to sail home but, as you mentioned before, he might have decided never to set foot in anything floating on water ever again!

'The company will be happy to foot the bill for his flight but I think now is the time to bring his lady friend into the equation.

'Why not contact her stewardess and say I'd like to speak to Mrs Brown as soon as possible?'

'Great! Shall I do that straight away?'

'By all means.'

Back at the desk Carys looked up

Lucy's cabin number then found the extension number she needed. She was assured the chief's message would be relayed.

About a half hour later Lucy was talking to Andy in his office. He had asked Carys to be present.

There were indeed tears, though tears of joy. Andy proffered a box of man-size tissues while Carys pretended not to be at all affected by Lucy's obvious joy.

'I can't wait to see him!' Lucy cried. 'I'm already booked on the eleven o'clock launch so I can take a taxi to the hospital and back again.'

'Are you happy to go alone?' Andy asked her gently.

'Oh, yes, thank you. More than happy.'

Andy explained that they needed to know whether Simon was prepared to rejoin *The Golden Goddess* and assured her that a flight would be booked should he feel unable to do so.

'I may as well tell you that the man who was with him when he went overboard won't be returning to the ship.

'He'll be flown back to the UK to attend a court hearing. I'll be sending with you a letter to ensure Mr Waters is aware of this.

'Perhaps you'll call for it at the desk before you leave. It will also assure him of his freedom to choose how he returns home.'

'If he doesn't want to rejoin the ship I'll ask if he'd like me to fly back with him,' Lucy told Carys after they left Andy. 'I'll be happy to pay my own air fare.'

'That's wonderful, Lucy. He's a lucky man in more ways than one!'

'If he feels about me as I feel about him there won't be two happier or luckier passengers, either on the ship or on the aeroplane.'

She gave Carys a swift hug.

'I'll call for that letter later. Thanks so much for all your support.'

What a wonderful start to the day, Carys thought.

The moment she got the opportunity she'd ring the stewardesses' number again to ask if they had any news from Tina about Summer.

★ ★ ★

Noah was hovering in the foyer as Carys neared the end of her shift. He caught her eye and saw her expression change first to surprise, then to uncertainty.

His heart went out to her. His timing had been badly off when he'd asked whether she might consider a change of gear in their relationship. How stupid had that been?

The trouble was this girl was in his thoughts so often these days. He fell asleep thinking of her, hoping he'd dream about her.

He woke up and saw her face smiling up at him while raindrops pattered on their heads and neither of them took the least bit of notice.

She was walking towards him now.

'Hello, Noah.'

'Hello, yourself,' he replied, restraining himself from taking her in his arms.

'You're probably going to hate me for this but I've booked us both a place on the next launch. 'I'm afraid it means you don't have time to change out of uniform but, well, I thought it might be nice if we got away from the ship for at least a couple of hours.'

He couldn't stop gazing at her and cursed himself for acting like a lovesick swain in some Shakespearean drama. Well, he could certainly play that rôle, given his feelings.

But what if she turned him down now, leaving him to go ashore on his own and at the mercy of the passengers?

These lovely people might be his bread and butter but he'd rather sing in front of twelve hundred theatregoers than attempt polite conversation with a dozen passengers in a launch.

To his amazement, although she looked solemn she was nodding.

'Yes. One of us needs to make a decision so thanks for this.

'As it happens my colleague Suzanne advised me to keep a casual outfit in the office, to save going back to my cabin if ever I needed to change. I can be ready in plenty of time.'

Brave Summer

Summer, wearing a silky green kimono embroidered with blue butterflies, sat drinking strong coffee. Tina was in a chair opposite her on the balcony.

Summer was too calm for her liking. She'd informed her manager, who let the purser's office know that the Maitlands' very experienced stewardess was keeping Mrs Maitland company until she felt certain she could be left alone.

'I don't usually talk to people like this.' Summer drained her cup and set it down. 'But we've really taken to you, Tina. Are you quite sure you won't hand in your notice and become my personal assistant after we reach Southampton?

'Whatever the cruise company pays you I'll increase it!'

Tina chuckled.

'It's a very tempting offer, Mrs Maitland.'

'Call me Summer, darling!'

'Thanks but, Summer, your husband

237

could be released on bail. He might even be freed in time to join you on the return trip.'

Summer rolled her eyes.

'Who knows? I rang his lawyer so the wheels will be turning but, after all, this is Christmastime. The ship will set off on the homeward voyage come Boxing Day with or without my husband on board.

'Some special birthday celebration this has turned into!'

She frowned at her empty cup.

'I'll fetch a top up, shall I?' Tina headed for the kitchenette.

'Thank you, darling. Then come back and tell me all about your lovely man. How do you manage to conduct a romance with such odd hours and so many pairs of eyes?'

'With difficulty!' Tina called.

Again her charge seemed amazingly calm. Would she crack? It was hard to tell.

She heard the phone ring and almost immediately Summer answered it.

When Tina returned, bearing coffee,

Summer was inspecting her nails.

'I've just learned my husband will have to fly back to London as soon as possible.'

'Oh, I'm so sorry. Will you go, too?'

'No. I have my writing to keep me occupied and I don't intend giving up this suite until we reach Southampton.

'Rupert will probably be granted bail in due course. Now, you can help keep my mind off this horrible business by telling me about you and the chief purser.'

'Oh, goodness! There's not much to tell, really. We've known each other a while but it was only on our last cruise that Andy confessed his feelings.'

'Darling, that's so sweet! You've given me an idea for a feature about finding love on the ocean wave.' She chuckled. 'It'll occupy me while I'm in solitary confinement.'

'No-one's locking you in your suite, Summer. You might like to see the friends who came to your birthday, for instance.'

Summer's snort was unladylike.

'Purely business buddies of my

husband. Not one of their wives has half as much about her as you do, darling, or even that little Welsh girl at Reception! Has she found romance on board, by any chance?'

'I couldn't say. I don't want to be the one to start tongues wagging. Shipboard rumours spread like chocolate in the hands of a two-year-old.'

Summer laughed.

'I might steal that expression for my feature! Tina, promise me, if you won't come and work for me, that you and your handsome lover will dine with me one evening while I'm still on my own.'

'I can't speak for Andy as he sometimes dines with the captain or the staff captain, but I'd be delighted to join you for dinner. And if I hear of any more shipboard romances I'll let you know.

'No names mentioned, of course!'

The journalist sighed.

'Between you and me, darling, I'm thankful I have my career to fall back on. It would have been so easy to let my husband pay for everything while I swanned around doing very little at all.

'I'm even wondering whether to begin on that novel I keep threatening to write.'

'That sounds very positive. Will you still go to the creative-writing sessions?'

Summer shrugged.

'I don't know. I'll maybe ask Willoughby Franks if he'd like to have lunch with me some time. We get on well but I'm not sure I can face too many people at the moment.'

Tina leaned forward.

'You're a brave lady. Don't let this get you down. It's a difficult time but you have people who care about you.

'I know very little about your husband's situation, but I do see how much he loves you. He'll need your support now, more than ever before.'

Summer swallowed hard.

'How kind you are. You've cheered me up already. I do love Rupert, you know. But he needs teaching a lesson, that's for sure.'

White Keys

Noah and Carys were in the same launch as Mark and his girlfriend. He gave her a knowing grin when he spotted her and mouthed 'Hooray!' while the singer was looking back at the liner.

Noah was subdued and making no attempt to hold her hand. How could she blame him? He hadn't meant to hurt her but she needed to explain her feelings when they had their private chat.

The launch reacted to a choppy section of water. Noah put his arm around her and hugged her close without saying a word.

She wanted to nestle against him but, as usual, there was more than one person looking their way. She prayed nobody would whistle or call out some teasing comment.

Yet, if she really loved him, why should she give two hoots about the rest of the world's opinion?

'You're on tenterhooks, I can tell.' He

removed his arm as the launch nosed towards the jetty. 'Let's find a quiet café and get shot of that elephant in the room!'

She nodded.

'Carys,' he whispered. 'Whatever choice you make will be the right one. Whatever I might think or want I'll go along with your decision. Fair enough?'

'Fair enough,' she repeated, hoping she sounded calmer than she felt.

As soon as they stepped ashore Noah and Carys made their way to the town square and soon found a café in an alley leading off the centre.

Lush greenery wound itself round wrought-iron railings. Terracotta pots trailed crimson blossoms on to grey paving stones.

Noah ordered cold drinks and they decided to move inside where it was quieter, sitting at the rear and admiring stunning island paintings on the walls.

Noah took a sip of his iced lime and lemon concoction.

'Fruit juices always taste so much

better when the fruit hasn't far to travel.'

'I'm fast learning that.'

Carys had chosen fresh pineapple juice, the cheerful young man behind the counter having taken much pleasure in telling them how White Keys was in its second harvesting season of the year and that she would find the taste sublime.

'Shall I hold your hand while you give me my marching orders or not?'

Oh, no! Her heart was bumping fast enough as it was! She needed to keep her wits about her and not be influenced by his squeezing her fingers or kissing her palm.

'Thank you for being so understanding.'

She saw him nod, his gaze fixed on her.

'Noah, I'm contracted to work another two cruises after this one. I'll be in no position to spend much time with you, wherever you are in the world.'

She sighed.

'But from the moment I saw you that day at Southampton something happened. I must admit I fought against it.

'What was I thinking of? Signing on for my first cruise, having been accepted for a rôle I'd only ever dreamed of obtaining. No way was I looking for romance that day until Fate decided otherwise.'

He was still gazing at her, staying quiet to let her have her say.

He looked so gorgeous she almost crumbled. Almost told him she would ask whether her contract could be cancelled so that she could go back to working on dry land as soon as the company released her.

But no. She'd made her decision.

Carys reached for Noah's hands and he held them out willingly. She clasped them tightly and sent that elephant in the room packing.

The Right Decision

Lucy followed the young nurse along the corridor. The soles of the nurse's shoes squeaked as she trod the linoleum and Lucy had to try not to giggle from nerves.

What if he didn't remember her? She couldn't bear it if that should be the case.

The nurse stopped outside a half-open door and peered around it.

'You have a visitor, Mr Waters.' She pushed the door further open. 'I'll collect you after twenty minutes unless he's not too tired and wants you to stay longer.'

Lucy could have listened to the nurse's melodious voice all day but she nodded and went inside the room.

Martin — no, Simon — was sitting up in bed and was smiling at her. She could hear birdsong through the open window.

'Lucy! You can't imagine how good it is to see you.'

She didn't care whether the cheerful Caribbean nurse was watching or not. She leaned forwards and kissed him on the lips.

'Hello, Mr Miracle Man. I can't find words to tell you how much I've missed you.'

He reached out his hand.

'Please sit beside me. I owe you an explanation, my dear. I hope I haven't caused you too much distress.

'Believe me, I never intended to jump into the sea!'

Lucy sank on to the chair.

'I don't want to bring back bad memories but you should know the man with you that night has been taken into custody.

'If you're well enough to join *The Golden Goddess* for the homebound voyage he definitely won't be on board.'

She handed him the letter.

Simon nodded.

'I hope to sail back with you if you can forgive me for taking an assumed name. My original passport is locked in my suitcase.

'Can you tell me how the police got involved?'

'You need to talk to a girl called Carys.'

* * *

'Are you absolutely sure about this?'

'Positive.'

'Fantastic!' Noah's voice echoed round the quiet little café.

Two people choosing drinks at the bar looked round, startled, but Carys and Noah had eyes only for one another.

'I really thought you were giving me my marching orders,' he confessed.

'How could I have done that? The decision was easy as soon as I realised how much I loved you. Ours won't be a normal relationship but somehow we'll manage.'

'We will! I love you, too, Carys, so much. Shall we drink up and head out of here? Unless you want me to take you in my arms and kiss you in front of everyone!'

They finished their drinks and left, hand in hand, strolling along until they came to a small park. Noah led her to a bench hidden beneath the branches of a tree whose feathery leaves formed the perfect shelter.

He kissed her lightly on the mouth once before taking her in his arms and kissing her until all she wanted was for the moment to go on and on.

At last he released her and they sat cuddled together behind the leafy green screen, discussing ways to make their relationship work.

'Andy and Tina are determined to stay together even though Andy works far longer hours than she does. And Mark and his girlfriend seem to manage.

'But both these couples work on the same ship. My fear is being parted from you for long periods.'

She hesitated.

'I don't want to break my contract, Noah. And, even if I could, I wouldn't ask you to let me tag along with you wherever you end up next.'

'You mustn't worry about anything, Carys. We have the rest of this cruise to look forward to and we'll spend as much time as possible together.'

'I daren't ask for extra leave before my next cruise as I'm still a novice,' she fretted.

He silenced her with another kiss.

'Don't think of the negatives, my darling, just the positives. Trust me. I'm considering my career options.

'For now let's enjoy being together and let the future take care of itself.'

He reached inside his rucksack and produced a tiny box.

She gasped when he revealed the turquoise ring she'd so admired on their first trip ashore.

He slipped it on the little finger of her right hand.

'This is to help you remember how we met. I hope, one day, to give you a ring with a much more significant meaning.'

Carys knew she had made the right decision. Couples throughout the ages had coped with being parted from one another.

So many women faced long separations when their fiancés and husbands were posted overseas.

Even though their relationship was in its early stages she already knew the bond between Noah and herself was strong.

As if he'd read her mind, she heard him whisper in her ear.

'We have the rest of our lives to look forward to.'